I blow on the candle – gently at first, to watch the shadows dance across the dome where all the bricks go spiralling around and up in perfect ordered rows, circle on circle any way you look. Then harder puffs, and harder, until the ice house loses its warm and rounded shape and looks as fantastical, as full of crags and strange deceptive hollows, as one of those cold ancient caverns, miles underground.

I blow too hard. The flame tips over suddenly, in trouble, tries a quick wiggle to right itself, then disappears with a soft pop. The ice house turns cold and dark and small again, and there is nothing left to do but follow Jamieson alone.

Cass hasn't come . . .

aNNe FiNe

Round Behind the
Ice House

For Claudia,
with love,

Anne Fine

CORGI BOOKS

ROUND BEHIND THE ICE HOUSE
A CORGI BOOK 0 552 55268 2
978 0 552 55268 4 (from January 2007)

First published in Great Britain in 1981 by Methuen Children's Books Ltd
Published in Penguin Books 1990
Updated edition published by Corgi Books 2006

1 3 5 7 9 10 8 6 4 2

Set in 12/16pt Gioconda by
Falcon Oast Graphic Art Ltd.

Corgi Books are published by Random House Children's Books,
61–63 Uxbridge Road, London W5 5SA,
a division of The Random House Group Ltd,
in Australia by Random House Australia (Pty) Ltd,
20 Alfred Street, Milsons Point, Sydney, NSW 2061, Australia,
in New Zealand by Random House New Zealand Ltd,
18 Poland Road, Glenfield, Auckland 10, New Zealand,
and in South Africa by Random House (Pty) Ltd,
Isle of Houghton, Corner Boundary Road & Carse O'Gowrie,
Houghton 2198, South Africa

THE RANDOM HOUSE GROUP Limited Reg. No. 954009
www.kidsatrandomhouse.co.uk

A CIP catalogue record for this book is available from the British Library.

Printed and bound in Great Britain by
Cox & Wyman Ltd, Reading, Berkshire

For my sisters

Chapter 1

Till the summer Cass changed, I had always had someone to be with. There had always been Cass. She'd be there with me, crouching down deep in the hedge at the end of the lane, watching Jamieson set up the steel traps we sprang every evening as soon as he'd gone, or back at the farm while I tackled the homework and she fed the chickens, or I fed the chickens as she did the homework.

Or down at the ice house, curled up on the sacks, writing some new fault down on The List.

The List was impressive by then. We had started it years before – almost as soon as we learned how to write – in a huge silver scrapbook Aunt Nina had sent us one Christmas. When we tore off the wrappings I felt disappointed, for all that it looked so bright, stiff and untouched, and the paper smell still hung around it. I couldn't see how a scrapbook could be shared, even by twins: her sprawling girly patterns in the front, my football cards in the back?

I needn't have worried, for Cass thought of something. (She usually does.) Her first plan was a contest between us to see who was 'worst'. Only things that grown-ups said were counted, and not if they criticized both of us at the same time, since as often as not that just meant that they weren't really looking, Cass told me.

I got *messy, untidy, forgetful* and *clumsy* the very first day, and Cass managed *quarrelsome, bossy* and *rude* for herself. They were spelled rather strangely, it's true, and the *e*'s and the *s*'s faced backwards on some of my words; but the start of The List can be read still quite clearly. At six, we pressed hard and wrote big.

The contest part ended quite soon. We'd both realized we had very different failings down in the columns under each of our names. But it was Cass who first thought of cheating, and quite deliberately one morning slopped streaks of filthy paint water over the rim of her jam jar onto the rug, so that she could get *messy*, and creep one fault further ahead.

Cass never spills anything, even if tripped. I knew what she was up to at once. I was furious. Snatching the jar from her hand, I went stamping around on the damp marks she'd made. I was trying to tread them all in.

What little paint water was left in the jar flew out and up in giant shining globules, and landed on everything.

'Thomas! Don't get so *excitable*!' Mum shouted through the half-open door to the kitchen. 'You'll wear a great hole in the rug!'

So I spoiled the trick after all, and poor Cass never did once get *messy*. But that day we pooled both the lists in a communal effort to get to one hundred. (*Excitable* was sixty-six.)

All that was a long time ago. The huge silver scrapbook's been filled up for years. We're on one of Mum's order books now, a red Size 3 Eggs one, on page forty-seven, with twenty-two lines on each page.

It's more interesting too, now we're older. This morning, for example, I overheard Dad grumbling, 'Whenever I see Cass these days, the girl's staring mindlessly into a mirror.' I thought I would go to the ice house to write the criticism in for her and, just as I walked through the kitchen, I picked up the exact reverse from Mum:

'You *never* look into a mirror, Tom, do you? Not even before you go out.'

It's not just that they fault us differently. It's also as if, to grow as twins, we chose to split ourselves in two right from the start, failings and skills. And now some things are mine and some are Cass's for better or worse. If I fell in the combine-harvester, she'd probably have to live for ever with her unslippy slip-knots, unable to tell when an animal's sick just from taking a good look, and never able to close the barn doors since, with me there, she hasn't ever bothered to master the knack of rocking them over the warps on the floor.

And it's the same for me. If Cass ran away from the farm, would I go through the rest of my life unsure which pair of boots are mine until she's reached for hers, hopeless at changing bulbs in the cowshed lights, and never brave enough to answer Mum back the way that Cass can now?

Maybe I wouldn't stay a half-person long. After

all, if through the years I've grown in and out of some of my own faults, surely I could grow into some of Cass's if I chose – especially the commonest ones, the ones that we heard about over and over.

There was a time when we kept track of those. We used to add them up in neat sets of ten, and then Cass (who was still in the top maths group then) used to run up brightly coloured block graphs every now and again. The counting was tedious, though, so we stopped when my *untidy* and Cass's *selfish* and *slapdash* had been out in front for two years. Of course, everything's changed. There's been *moody* and *rude* for Cass endlessly since, and I've heard them whispering, 'Tom's got so *secretive*,' such a lot more than they used to, and bellowing, 'Don't be so *noisy*, Tom!' such a lot less.

We had a sort of ritual for adding a new fault onto The List, Cass and I. We would sigh very heavily all of the time that it took to write in, then:

'Ah, well. Nobody's perfect,' I'd say very gravely, and slide the book back in its two plastic bags before wrapping the tinfoil around it.

'Very true,' Cass would nod. 'Very true.'

And then, when we'd stopped laughing, she'd roll off the sacking so I could reach over to shove The List back in its hiding place.

'Ready?' she'd say, and she'd blow out the candle, and we would go home for our supper and 'You two have been in that filthy old hole in the ground again, haven't you? Oh, you are silly! It will fall in and kill you one day.'

Cass only shrugged. After all, '*silly*' is down on the very first page of the scrapbook, and she can't be bothered with old ones. So I'd reassure Mum.

'No, no. It's quite safe. It won't fall.'

And it won't, for the ice house is beautifully built. It will never fall in. From outside it looks just like a small rounded hummock sprawled over with cowslips and nettles and ground ivy, deep in the spinney. You'd think someone once dumped a cartload of fresh brown damp earth there and everything growing around just spread over in no time at all.

At the front, we've encouraged the brambles. Cass and I started trailing them over the brickwork a long time ago, and by now they're so thick and unkempt that you can't see the entrance at all from outside in the summer. Each early spring, the scrabbling, trailing growths of every colour from almost yellow to almost black mat themselves into one another even more stiffly than the year before. In June, a huge malevolent convolvulus trumpets white triumph over them all. And by July, this place has grown so dank and thick and private that only if I stand right by the entrance, leaning hard back against the crumbling brickwork so that it bites my skin through my thin shirt, can I see out through all the twists and tangles. You'd never guess, if you were standing just a few steps away from me outside, that I was standing here, watching you.

This place is like an echoing underground igloo, built out of small dark red bricks. The tunnel entrance is pitted and worn from weather now; yet where, a short way in, it suddenly widens out to a large dark dome, the brickwork is still glossy and strong.

Once the ice house was very much deeper. They kept all the game that was killed on the big estate stored down here, month after month. They ferried shock-eyed leggy deer and piles of pheasants along the river to the landing stage a little way down the slope outside. They hauled them up on wooden sleds, and packed them away in straw between the massive blocks of ice brought down from the north.

Since then, someone's filled up the ice house with earth. Whoever it was has dug load after load from the edge of the copse. You can still see the weeds grow in scallops along the wide pit where it came from. Of course, Jamieson told us they filled in the pit because a child died down here, breaking her leg as she landed, not able to scrabble her way up the sides to get out.

'Do you believe him?' I remember asking Cass.

'Of course not, stupid!' (Even to think about Jamieson used to make Cass turn fierce.) 'It's just the sort of thing he likes to make up when he's setting traps.'

So the ice house is more like a cave than a pit now. It has that same wet bricky feel you get in unused railway tunnels, and gritty crumbs fall in your hair every now and again. Cass and I put the sacking floor in by ourselves, and we used to go halves on the candles.

We spent most of our time here in summer. We only went home for our meals, or to sleep. If they asked where we'd been, we'd say 'up in the hay-barn' or 'round by the cowsheds'. If they pinned us down, saying Jamieson saw us run off to the river, we'd say we were playing about by the old bridge, or climbing the trees in the spinney. We would never admit we were down at the ice house.

I still do that now. If they ask me, I always imply that I made for the river, though no one gets anxious about where I am when I'm out of the house, now I'm older.

As for Cass, it just doesn't arise any more, for she rarely comes down to the ice house with me. Though The List's getting longer, it's me who writes all the new faults in. (To give Cass her due, for the most part they're hers.)

If I ask her, she says, 'Not right now. Maybe later.'

So I wander off, and come down here, and hope that she'll follow. But Cass hardly ever appears. As I told you, she's changed.

I write in the back of this red Size 3 Eggs book until I'm quite sure she's not coming. Then I slide it back with the scrapbook inside the bags and wrap them up tightly again. That's when I miss her most, her not being there to say, 'Very true. Very true,' and laugh with me when I say, 'Nobody's perfect.'

Then the ice house seems horribly lonely. The tin foil always crackles as I fold it, and when the creases catch the candlelight they flicker fire colours over the brickwork, making the packet feel hard and chilly in my fingers for all those sudden reds and oranges. I lay it down inside its hiding place and drop two heavy bricks back down on top, cutting the packet's last tiny glitterings off as if it were a campfire that I'd been sitting by alone, and just stamped out.

I blow on the candle – gently at first, to watch the shadows dance across the dome where all the bricks go spiralling around and up in perfect ordered rows, circle on circle any way you look. Then harder puffs, and harder, until the ice house loses its warm and rounded shape and looks as fantastical, as full of crags and strange deceptive hollows, as one of those cold ancient caverns, miles underground.

I blow too hard. The flame tips over suddenly, in trouble, tries a quick wriggle to right itself, then disappears with a soft pop. The ice house turns cold and dark and small again, and there is nothing left to do but follow Jamieson alone.

Cass hasn't come.

We used to follow Jamieson together. It was more fun. To tell the truth, I wouldn't bother now, except that over the years that we've been doing it I've come to care about the following in just the way that Cass did when we started but doesn't any longer.

Jamieson goes killing things the whole day long. It's practically his job here on the farm. It's certainly the only thing we ever hear him talking about. And Cass believes that it's a little hobby of his, when he gets home. She's got some amazing things down on The List for saying so, like *vicious little gossip-monger* and *bitch*, and she's been ticked off often enough by Dad. But still she maintains that every creature who ever died on this farm was poisoned by Jamieson. Even while he's taking off his boots in the scullery, I'll hear her accusing whisper:

'You know that barn owl that stopped hooting? I reckon that was him.'

And once, without even looking round to

check that Lisa wasn't there to hear: 'Remember when Lisa's mother walked out on Jamieson all those years ago? Somebody should have mentioned it to the police. They might have found a body, if they'd looked hard enough.'

She hates the man with such a flaming passion that she won't speak to him. That isn't easy when we all eat together twice a day, but Cass has managed it for six years now. If he sits down beside her, she shifts very slightly on the bench, again and again, until she's politely turned her back on him, but can't be accused of flouncing around.

We all know perfectly well what's going on – especially Jamieson. He persecutes Cass quite deliberately. He waits, with his back wedged up against the draining board, his jacket trailing in that stale furry water that gathers underneath the plate rack, standing quite still in the way only he can stand still. He tilts his head a little to the side, as if he were listening, and strands of his black greasy hair fall over his face. Then, when Mum's made poor Cass sit down, he breaks into that leering gappy smile of his and slouches towards whichever space at the table is opposite Cass.

That way, he traps her, like he traps everything.

Sometimes he kills the things he catches. Sometimes he uses them. He caught a full-grown seagull once, a gorgeous wheeling seagull that landed in his cottage garden early one spring, in fierce winds. He kept it crushed inside a wicker basket for hours and hours, blinking and heaving in panic, while Cass and I begged him to let it go again and Lisa stood behind him, so close to tears.

He listened to us patiently, grinning away to show his black gaps, and picking at his jacket. And afterwards he cut the seagull's wings right across in such a way that it couldn't fly any more, ever.

'As soon as you'd gone,' Lisa told us, months after. 'He did it as soon as you'd gone.'

And till it died, two winters later, that seagull had to waddle round Jamieson's vegetable plots like a duck someone drew a bit wrong and painted the wrong colours, eating the insects and slugs, keeping the lettuces nice for market. Poor Lisa had to watch it.

Cass hasn't spoken to him since he did that. And neither of us ever again went far down the footpath that leads to Jamieson's cottage.

But Cass invented 'following' round about then.

Chapter 2

'Tom. Thomas! *Tom!*'

I sat quite still on the high wall above the greenhouses, waiting for Mum to give up on me, and switch to calling Cass instead.

'Thomas! Where are you? *Thomas!*'

As Jamieson crossed the yard behind her, he said:

'No use in yelling for that boy. Cloth-eared, Tom is, and he gets worse.'

I almost spoke up then, to spite him; but I was far too close to them. They would have known I'd been there all the time.

'Cass. Cass! *Cassandra!*'

She poked her head out of her bedroom window at once.

'I'm busy *doing* something. What do you *want?*'

It still gives me a shock to hear her calling back at them, when they call her. Time was when neither she nor I would rustle a leaf when we were called – but that was when we were together, following.

We took it seriously, prepared to wait for hours wedged, chilled and cramped, in dripping trees, or squatting in flooded ditches, till Jamieson would finally stride off, satisfied, and we could move in. He uses poisons and sprays and gases and traps, and even an unlicensed gun that his grandfather kept back at the end of the war, so it's always been dangerous to follow him, and we were forbidden by Dad to go anywhere near him while he was on jobs. Dad meant it, too. We knew right from the start that if we were ever caught at it, we'd be in deep, deep trouble.

But Cass said we must. And Lisa, though she dared not help, never told. And so together Cass and I sprang the vicious little traps we'd watched Jamieson positioning with such skilled care. We flicked small pebbles that would spin away afterwards at their steel hair-springs. We scraped the rough grey pellets of poisoned bait that he'd been scattering back into one tidy lethal little pile, and buried them deep, along with the sticks we'd used to gather them and dig the hole. Oh, we were very careful, right from the start. We'd seen enough of Jamieson's successes not to run risks.

We followed him for days on end sometimes in spring, his busiest, most savage season. We passed whole weeks as outlaws or resistance workers, guerrillas or spies. I even remember being a wolf-child once. It was so much more fun, then.

I follow him alone now. The worst is moles. Jamieson hates moles in just the same way as Cass hates him. I don't hate anyone or anything like that, and sometimes I've wondered if there's a sort of hole in me where that feeling gets into them. I've come to the edges of hating sometimes, but that's as far as it goes. I truly believe that Jamieson's disgusting. I don't like anything he says or does. I don't like to think that he works on this farm, which I'll run one day, and that every field and thicket around will seem haunted by him for ever. If he weren't Lisa's father I'd wish him a hundred miles away. He doesn't make me boil, though. I wouldn't get into trouble over him, day after day, like Cass does. I can't imagine hating like that.

But Cass has always been hot-headed. *Spitfire*, Dad calls her, and leaves the room when she starts up; but she and Mum wrangle on for hours just like this morning, in the yard, with Cass halfway to falling out of her bedroom window, and Mum shaking the mop at her, furious.

'I don't see why I should. Why *should* I?'

'Because I say so.'

'That isn't fair!'

'Now, listen, young lady—'

But Cass was howling her down already:

'You can't *say* that. "Because I say so." I'm not a *child*!'

'I'm warning you, Cass . . .'

I shifted further along the wall towards Jamieson, under cover of all the noise they were making, still safe out of his sight since he's one of those people who never look up, and I watched him dig in that calm and methodical way of his. Whenever he spotted an earthworm just over-turned by the flat of his spade into sunlight, and curling around on itself, or the tip of a stir in the earth where he'd brought down the blade just a moment before, he leaned over and prised it away from the clods of damp earth it was clinging to with such a slow gentle touch you would think he was rescuing them, and not dropping them into the battered old bucket that stood right beside him. I knew why Jamieson wanted those earthworms. He uses them as bait for the moles.

When he thought he'd enough, he went back to his shed, whistling softly, and left me alone staring down at the bucket and wishing that Cass were beside me, not pointlessly fighting with Mum in the yard.

Cass would have leaped down from the wall right then, and run with the ghastly bucket of writhing, slithering earthworms along the path to where the long grass starts. She'd tip them out to disappear slowly but silently. Then she'd hare back and dump the bucket down upon its side, exactly where he'd left it.

'There!' she'd say. 'That'll show him. *Butcher!*'

She'd hope that Jamieson would blame the dogs, or think that he'd taken longer than he had back at the shed, or that the worms that he'd picked out were racing worms, or something. Cass often acts as if everyone's an idiot except herself; but I can't work like that against Jamieson, not any more.

That was fine till a few months ago. Oh, he'd guess what we'd done just as soon as he shambled back round the greenhouse corner and saw his precious bucket tipped over on the grass.

'*Wretches!*' he'd snarl. '*Brats!*'

And he'd know why we'd done it, as well. But Dad would put it down to mischief or clumsiness or thoughtlessness, and Jamieson would be forced to agree, for we were still too young then even for Jamieson to declare outright war on us both.

It's different now. I realized, watching them one afternoon as she stalked out as he came in, that Cass has grown taller than Jamieson. And I've grown just taller than Cass. So I can't do things that way any longer. He wouldn't take it from me. He doesn't have to back down any more, now that I'm taller than he is.

Of course, I can get him in the end. That's settled. Cass tells me all the time: 'You can have my half of the farm. But only if the first thing you do is order that man off our land.'

So I will sack him. I won't even let him work his notice out. I shall just pay him off. (I wouldn't like to be any wild animal this side of Fretley the last month that Jamieson works.)

But right now, it's as if I'm paralysed. There's nothing I can do. I still keep following him. I don't know why. I go on silently watching him from high on walls and through the cracks in stable doors. I work out endless complicated plans of sabotage and rescue that I don't dare to carry out. It all has to die. I watch it die. I can't save anything.

Cass could, since she's a girl; but she won't even come any more. He wouldn't dare take on Cass. He knows as well as we do that up until Christmas she was taller than me, and stronger. She's always been cleverer. But Jamieson wouldn't touch her all the same, since she's a girl. He knows that Dad would jump on him if he did. If Jamieson started on me, Dad would be there on the sidelines, silently willing me on to smash his face in, out of good old family loyalty; but he would never interfere. He'd never lay a finger on Jamieson on my behalf, or tell him to leave. He'd say:

'Cross a man who's simply doing his job, and take what you get, Tom. That's my advice.'

And it is Jamieson's job to kill pests, I suppose, along with repairing broken fences and reslating sheds and clearing drainage ditches. But moles aren't pests, unless you have a perfect clip-edged square of lawn you mow every other Sunday morning, and shoo other people's children off, and stroll around every now and again, fretting about the thin patches under the washing line, and proud of the lush green thick bits. Then, fair enough, if a family of moles moved in, and threw up their little brown messy mountains all over the place, you might call them pests. But here on a farm, way down in the apple orchard or round by the barns, I'd say they were just moles.

Jamieson comes out with his reasons time and again at the table. It torments poor Cass. She glares down at her plate so fiercely you think all the dishes and glasses around her will crack.

'Their runs disturb the young plant roots,' Jamieson grouses. 'Those molehills will damage the blades of my mower. Did you know that they eat up good earthworms?' There's no end to the things he thinks up. He's interested in them, I have to admit. He knows more about moles than anyone else in the world, I should think. He told us one day a mole's penis points backwards, and offered to show us, but we ran away. For years I assumed it was just one of Jamieson's tales, till

I saw for myself on a body he'd left in his bucket.

I'd scooped the soft black limp thing out with a stick, because you can't touch anything that's been in that bucket or you'd end up dead too. I remember the dull quiet unwanted thud that it made as it flopped on the grass, and I felt sick and sad and I very much wanted to hold it, but couldn't of course. Moles are lovely to hold. They've got small pointed muzzles, the tiniest eyes, and their ears are so small you don't notice at first that they have them. Their short stand-up fur doesn't go any way in particular, so that however you stroke them they feel smooth as bathwater under your fingers. They squeak at you all the time that you've got them. You can't hold them long.

I flipped it over on the grass out of sudden curiosity. I wanted to be perfectly sure that Jamieson was wrong. I feel that way often. It's something to do with not wanting the world to be anything like the way Jamieson sees it. I flattened down the bulging fur and felt bad about it, as if by spread-eagling the dead mole on its back just to peer at it, I might be hurting it all over again. The claws on its small paddle legs scraped up the rough edge of the stick, and I let go, startled. But I had seen that Jamieson was right, so now I have to believe him whenever he says over supper that moles can be frightened to death with a tap on the nose, or a very loud noise like his ringing the side of his bucket with anything metal, or simply by leaving them in there for less than a day, since a mole starves to death within hours. He's probably right. He's done it himself in his time, I'm quite sure. But he poisons them now, with his worm bait.

The way he prepares it is sickening. You'd think he'd have to hate worms quite as much as he hates moles to get the job done. He sprinkles poisonous dust all over them, and stirs them up. Can you believe it? Then he ambles off, whistling merrily, his ghastly bucket swaying at his side, down to the places where he knows the moles still run.

Anyone else in the world would find that they had to put the job off at this point. They wouldn't have the stomach to get through the next bit. I know my dad would say, 'There are so many heaps, I can't work out where the runs are,' and heel the soil down flat, and say he was waiting a few days to see where the new ones popped up.

Not Jamieson. I stand behind an apple tree and watch him stooping over the earth, taking his time, a horrid avenging angel. He can see tunnels through the very earth, or so it seems to me. He sees the whole pitch-dark living warren down there, the busy feeding burrows and deeper dwelling places. He knows at once that under here must be a main run leading along to water, but that branch there is simply a barely used off-shoot he can ignore. Sometimes I think he knows exactly where they are down there, diligently gobbling their grubs and larvae, just trying to stay alive.

As I move closer across the long grass, from apple tree to apple tree, he lays his instruments out beside his bucket, one by one, carefully. I know that he won't look round now and find me, he's much too absorbed: scissors, a clumsy dis-coloured wooden dibber, forceps, and some ancient rusting cocoa tin lid he's tipped a bit more of the poison-powder in, all ready for the next bit.

He bores a small hole down to the run with his dibber. It doesn't take long. And then with his forceps he picks out the first worm and holds it up high.

It's still alive, and I can see both ends of it, fresh-dusted grey, curl in the air in its last search for quiet and dampness and darkness and earth, before he snips the tip of its front end off with his scissors, and dips that raw cut into the cocoa tin lid, to dust that too. He stuffs the worm down the small hole he's made, and pushes it with the dibber till it falls into the run, where some busy burrowing unthinking mole will soon come across it. He blocks the hole up very tidily, with small soft kneaded balls of soil, then gathers his things together and moves on a little way. Then he bends down and does it all over again.

'Moles do it too,' we'll hear him insisting later over his lunch, in between dribbling spoonfuls of soup and snatching at rolls as the breadboard is passed round the table.

He'll see Cass's scornful dark eyes on him, and say it again. 'Moles do it too.'

He's right, of course. Moles do it. They bite the ends of earthworms that way, and store them alive but helpless – just the way Jamieson likes things – down in their runs until they decide to eat them.

And since my quarrel with Lisa, I've felt like

one of those worms. And that's how helpless she herself must have felt round behind the ice house the other day, when all the things I said made her cry, but so very quietly at first I didn't even notice, and just carried on with all of my hurting and hurting. I'd rather see anyone in the world cry than Lisa. So now I stand and watch her father at his sickening work, and when my stomach seizes up I tell myself: 'You stay and take it, Tom. It serves you right. You don't feel any worse than she did. You stay and take it.'

You can't pay things like that off though, however you try. I wish instead I could forget it all, go back and start the summer again. I wish I could. I wish I could.

Chapter 3

The summer started overnight, a blue and white explosion after so many weeks of still, quiet pond-green drizzle. Then every day was fierce light and frazzling heat, and all that squinting against the sun on the playing fields, and the soft warm dissolving feeling inside my bones as I sat with a book on the bus station railings after school felt foreign and strange, like somewhere else – Mexico, maybe.

They forced the sash windows up as far as they could in examination week. The dusty sunlight flooded in, and we could hear the lorries honking as far away as the bypass. The driver on the country bus that takes us home jammed his swing-open doors back to catch the breeze, and scowled at the cool, shirt-sleeved inspector who jumped on at Fretley roundabout in order to tell him to close them.

The next day he jammed them open again. That afternoon was even hotter. I sat in the seat behind Lisa and Cass and watched the peaky pale reflection of Lisa's face in the window as she stared out, fingering her wrists.

She's very thin – too thin, my dad says. He claims that her legs are really glass rods and he lifts her right up in his arms when he sees her 'in case she should stumble, and shatter'. He plays a game of 'feeding Lissie up' with titbits of sausage and cheese and rich fruit cake. He pops squares of food inside her mouth as if she were some fledgling starving inside an abandoned nest. It's only partly a joke, I think, for he never does it if Jamieson's there. Mum worries about Lisa, too. I've overheard her fretting to Dad about the blue shadows around Lisa's eyes and the way all her clothes just hang off her as if she were made out of wood.

She doesn't care. She doesn't care what she looks like. Lisa's not like Cass. She hacks at her hair with blunt rusty nail-scissors when it grows so long it gets into her eyes. It looks fluffy and chick-like at times (when she's washed it, Cass says), but the rest of the week it looks shredded. Her wrists and fingers are bluish, as if she were cold, yet summer and winter she wears the same clothes. Even in January she doesn't wear a duffel coat, though Mum has always sent the good ones Cass has outgrown home with Jamieson. Lisa sits by the door on the bus, under the stiff sliding windows that never fully close. Her feet slip out of her thin indoor shoes and brush against the icy ridges on the floor. She doesn't even shiver. And when the heat-waves start each summer she is the only one in the school to keep on her loose grey regulation sweater, however hot it becomes. The other girls whisper that it's because she has holes in her blouses under the arms; but I know that's not true. Though Mum makes me keep wearing my shirts till they wear deep grooves into my armpits, or mercifully fall apart, she always passes on Cass's blouses before they are even frayed much round the wrists.

Lisa looks odd, like a dusty spindly old-fashioned doll, whatever she wears. I like to sit behind her and Cass on the bus and watch the way her face changes in the glass as Cass reads their English homework aloud to her and she stares out of the window. They get through the set books much slower than you would imagine this way, for Lisa keeps having to tell Cass to read whole chunks over again, and as often as not she just misses them that time as well.

She fails practically all her exams every term. She just doesn't tell her father she sat them, and Jamieson never thinks to ask. We've noticed that Mum and Dad never mention schoolwork either, if Jamieson's there. For a while we thought it was just what they call 'not interfering', since Lisa does so badly; but now Cass and I know there's more to it than that: they don't want to embarrass Jamieson. Lisa let slip once that she reads and writes all her father's letters, and Halloran, who lives about a mile away behind their cottage, helps with confusing long forms. It seems that though Jamieson went to the old Fretley school for years and years, he never learned to read and write for himself. Halloran's offered to teach him, he says: but Jamieson always shakes his head. 'I'd only use it for the poisons,' he says. 'And I know them.'

So I could come home with a sheaf of bad marks and still know I was perfectly safe till

Jamieson left the farm after work. But only till then. You can see Mum and Dad getting more and more tense as they bottle their questioning up, out of tact. By the time Jamieson's gone they're both red-hot, especially towards the end of the term, with every examination result and final reports in each subject. The inquisition goes on all evening: 'How did you do so badly in this?' 'Whatever happened to you in that?' 'She says your work is *erratic*!' It's fault after fault to go down on The List. I'm so glad when the whole thing is over.

And then the term ends at last. Unused to having us around again on the farm, for a few days they leave us alone just so long as we keep well away from the work. But that never lasts long. Within a week or so we hear: 'Cass could make those cherry pies for you, surely. She's made them before, hasn't she?' And, seconds later: 'In fact, we could probably get that loose shedding fixed up by tonight, if Tom lends a hand.'

My eyes meet Cass's across the table, and both of us know that all we'll get from now on is a few hours every now and again, and bickering and bargaining for each hour longer, if we should

33

bother to ask them at all, and endless reminders to take my watch with us so we'll be quite sure to be back by the time that they said. I can't stand it. I'd just as soon be back at school where they leave you alone, if you don't count the bells and the whistles and shouts, and the signs pinned on every flat wall.

They don't last long, these first few days. So as soon as we can we leave the house, with bread and cheese and apples and cold greasy chunks of leftover meat stuffed inside plastic bags. Cass has the knack of knowing what we can take off pantry shelves or out of the fridge without Mum bothering. She can tell plums set aside for a crumble from plums Dad just happened to bring in last night, and good cheese they might have looked forward to eating from stale hard-edged cheese that they're glad to see gone. She can tell when a bone can start off another meal and when it can't. They all look like bones to me. I take her word for it. I always have. I tuck the food away under my arm, rolled up out of sight in a grimy old towel, and we creep out.

Each time we leave the house it's still so early the ground is grey with rising mist, and thick wet grasses slap at our ankles to make us gasp, like when they take us to the sea, and we've forgotten how cold sea is, we haven't been there for so long, and the ice burn of it on our feet makes us squeal like silly babies.

The spinney stays cool. The sunlight filters down through branches and leaves, and speckles and splatters the ground and the river and Cass and myself. It never gets baking sick hot like it can in the fields. We can hear Dad and Jamieson calling to one another at times, and the whirr of the tractor behind the big barns. We settle on the bank, where the river curls round behind the ice house, beside the old bridge. We have our own small oval patch of roll-flattened grass ready waiting, and a cool dark hole for our food in a rotted-out tree stump a few steps away.

Cass lies spread-eagled downwards on the towel and pulls threads from it with her teeth, munching them into small soggy balls and spitting them over the water. I sit beside her and watch them floating out of sight round the bend, and I chew all the juice out of one grass stalk after another. My clothes feel heavy and hot and cumbersome. The insects bother me, nosing, dive-bombing. I slap at them irritably, waiting for Lisa to come.

Lisa comes down every morning as soon as she can, as soon as she's done all the stupid petty little jobs her father thought up earlier, before he left for the farm. At least Dad decides that I'm to muck out pigs or mix feed or oil machines, real jobs that if I didn't do them then someone else would, since they obviously have to be done. Jamieson tells Lisa to do silly things like sweep all the twigs off a path no one uses, or count up the number of lettuces which will be ready for market next week, as if knowing would make any difference.

Mum says it would make a lot more sense if Jamieson told Lisa to cook a good nourishing meal for herself, or mend the hems on her clothes, or do her homework. But Jamieson doesn't seem to care about those things at all. Sometimes I think he doesn't care, either, about twiggy paths or half-grown lettuces, although he makes such a terrible fuss if Lisa skimps on the jobs he gives her. I think that for a short time every day he just likes to be giving orders, not taking them. It makes him feel better about things. If Lisa has to work too, for all that she's doing such daft little jobs, his own life doesn't seem so dreary.

So she's often a long time coming. But the other day, when we quarrelled, she was later than ever before. It was well after noon when she finally came. I had given her up, what with waiting and waiting, and hearing each rustle and twigsnap for hours, while Cass lay beside me, unruffled, asleep.

She stepped out into the sunlight between the squat clumps of bushes on the far side of the river, beside the bridge. She made no sound at all that I could hear. It was the flash of white from her school blouse that I saw first. Cass acts as if she'd sooner die on the rack than spend one hour longer than she has to in her school blouse, but Lisa couldn't care less. She wears it at weekends and on holidays, as if it were just some other shirt. That day she wore it untucked and half unbuttoned, although the sleeves were fastened at her wrists, and in her hand she held Dad's battered sun-hat, a great wide droopy straw affair she wheedled off him during haymaking last summer and never give back.

She looked so cool and happy and unhurried that just for a moment I felt hotter and crosser than ever, from having to wait so long for her to come. I watched her as she stretched out her hand and shook the wooden parapet, as if to see how feeble it was.

The bridge is rotten, through and through, and has been for years. Dad's always saying that it ought to come down, but Jamieson sometimes uses it as a short cut back home in bad weather. To cross, it's important to know where to put every step that you make, it's as dangerous as that.

The fretted decorative sides hang out at crazy looping angles far over the water, so you can't use them for support if you get stuck halfway across. You have to concentrate the whole way over, or you lose track of which of the boards in front of you can be trusted, and which will start to splinter even more under your weight.

She hesitated on the first board; but not, as I do, to run through the tricky counting rhyme Cass invented to make sure we start off the complicated crossing with the best foot. Instead Lisa swung herself up on the warped and trembling parapet, and stood there, upright and barefooted, her arms outstretched.

Scared to call out a warning and startle her into falling, I caught my breath. Cass heard me. She raised her head, and shielding her eyes against the glare, she watched with me as Lisa moved with a tightrope walker's slow sliding step along the parapet, which is horribly narrow and slopes so dangerously in the middle where all the fretwork leans away outwards in that uneven tired arc.

We watched in silence till she was over the straggling rushes alongside the bank. The river water is not dangerous or even very deep, except after storms; but still my hands were sticky, and all the time it was as if the spinney and Cass and myself had shrunk away out of sight and mind, and there was only Lisa up on the bridge.

She jumped to land on the firm earth bank. She'd crossed the bridge in half the time, with twice the ease, it ever took Cass or myself, and she still had the sun-hat in her hand.

'Show-off!' I heard Cass mutter at my side.

Lisa waved then, and called as she pushed

through the long grass to join us: 'Did you see that? Did you see me?'

'No,' I said. 'I didn't see.' Like Cass, I was cross.

'I saw.' Cass disconcerted me by adding, as if she'd never muttered 'Show-off!' at all: 'That was wonderful, Lisa. Amazing!'

So Lisa lay down beside Cass. We chewed and stewed for a while, till Lisa suddenly remembered:

'Guess what! I've got a summer job, sitting for Halloran.'

'A job? You mean Halloran's paying you for sitting? He's never paid me.'

'How much?' Cass asked.

'Four pounds an hour, from tomorrow morning, for just as long as it takes.'

'Four pounds an hour!' Cass scowled into the water. 'He's never paid *me* four pounds an hour!'

'He's never paid me a *penny*!'

Cass and I nursed our outrage together while Lisa hummed merrily, waiting. We've all sat for Halloran. Everyone round here has, at least once, including most of the more sluggish animals. He's never paid any of us. He says he has no money. Dad calls him a menace and acts as if Halloran were foot-and-mouth disease. He throws himself headlong into the nearest ditch whenever he sees him coming, and warns people when he's seen flashes of Halloran's scarlet jacket deep in the woods: 'Don't take that path. You'd better go the long way round, or you might run into Halloran.'

Halloran's a painter. Dad says there's one in every parish, it doesn't mean anything. But there have been exhibitions of Halloran's work in the Old Saxon Mill at Fretley, and the big county Art Gallery already has three of his paintings. The first one they bought was of me. *Sad Scarecrow*, Halloran called it. It wasn't very pleasant to sit for because he wouldn't let me sit down. He made me stand leaning backwards against some post he hadn't driven far enough into the ground. It wobbled badly the whole time, making me nervous. I asked him if I could lean against his doorway instead, but he said no. I had to keep my arms stuck out stiffly, but let my fingers flop at the ends. Halloran insisted on that. You try it. It's harder than you think, especially for days on end.

'It will be worth it,' Halloran kept comforting me whenever I complained. And so it was, for him. He was paid quite a lot of money for that painting, but he never gave me any.

Then Mrs Wheeler-Urquhart, who bought *Sad Scarecrow* for the Art Gallery, was heard to say on local radio she thought it the finest crucifixion painting she'd seen since her dear husband, the late Colonel Wheeler-Urquhart, exhibited his own *At The Third Hour.* Halloran stamped around threatening to buy *Sad Scarecrow* back from the Philistines; but since he'd spent practically all the money already, he couldn't. So I'm still hanging up there on the wall in that long room to the left of the Ladies. The upper school make regular field trips to see me. I don't know if they'll go on bothering after I leave.

Mum likes Halloran. She says he's trying, but nice. He's tall and thin and fierce-eyed, and about ten years younger than Dad, who claims to remember first hearing Halloran wailing, lost, down some long corridor in the old Fretley school. He says Halloran's the reason he left at fifteen, but we don't believe that, though Halloran is irritating if he's trying to get you to sit. He has this technique for getting sitters for nothing. He jumps on people and forces them into agreeing to do it. He won't let them go till they do. If they try walking off he simply follows them, and wails on and on about how much he needs them until they crack, or see the top deck of their bus weaving in and out between the hedges towards them. Then even the firmest refusers usually fix up a time very quickly because Halloran's been known to leap on the bus after people and then cadge the price of the fare.

'Now don't let me down!' Halloran yells after them. 'I'm depending on you.'

Most people forget the arrangement at once. Like Dad, they see Halloran simply as an obstacle to get past, like floods or wet tar, a sort of walking road hazard. But there are always a few, like Mum, who imagine him waiting, paintbrush lying ready, watching the hands on his Aunt Susan's clocks crawling round and round, disappointed and hurt. They go and sit for him every now and again when the feeling of guilt gets too much for them. More often they try to send somebody else. Convalescents and unwanted children are often packed off. 'Still sitting for Halloran?' is a way, around Fretley, of asking after somebody's health.

Cass and I started sitting while we were off

school with ringworm and Mum couldn't stand any more. 'It's neither or both,' she told Halloran firmly when she offered us.

Halloran took both, and as it turned out later, he got ringworm as well, for which he gained a certain dark respect around here. Dad says if a man will get ringworm for his painting, he'll stop at nothing; he's capable of kidnapping someone to sit for him, or digging up a fresh corpse and propping it up to sit for him till it rots. But Dad's been sour about Halloran since the night he was cornered in the Lamb and pinned down to a day and time in front of all his friends. When Halloran turned up at the farm two days later to see why Dad hadn't come as arranged, Dad bellowed across the hay field which he'd been working in since dawn that of *course* the sitting was off. Couldn't Halloran see there was *work* to be done?

'*Painting* is work!' Halloran wailed at him from over the hedge. (He doesn't like walking over the stubble. He says that the bits get into his socks.)

Dad swears he only said: 'Now don't be so silly, Halloran.' But Mum says she heard otherwise. Whatever it was, Halloran hasn't been near the farmhouse since. He still tramps quite happily over our land, frightening the sheep. (Mum says it's the colour of his jacket and Dad insists it's the way that he walks.) But Dad isn't keen on either of us sitting for Halloran any more. He always finds some good reason why it's better we don't: term-time, Aunt Sally's annual visit, dark before five; but we know it's more than that.

I'm sorry about it. I used to like sitting for Halloran, and so did Cass. She pestered Dad to change his mind much longer and harder than I did. So I was really surprised to hear her break off her brooding to say to Lisa: 'Tell Halloran I'm interested to hear he's paying four pounds an hour to his sitters now. Do tell him that might make a difference.' I don't see how it could make any difference. She knows how strongly Dad feels.

'He wants me especially,' Lisa told her proudly. 'He came round last night to ask about it. He's going in for some huge competition. He's quite convinced he'll win, if he can paint me. The prize is a great deal of money. I think that's the only reason he stayed when Dad told him I couldn't sit unless I was paid.'

She looked down. I think she was blushing. She

sounded as if she might be. It must be awful having Jamieson for a father – having to stand there and listen to yourself being bargained about like a lettuce with someone as poor as Halloran, whom no one else would dream of charging anything. Most people even take Halloran some food when they go and sit for him. (They know they won't get a thing to eat if they don't.) To get the promise of four pounds an hour out of Halloran, Jamieson must have haggled for hours.

'He wants to paint my hands,' Lisa said. 'Mine especially. I'm to sit with them in my lap. He kept saying that.' Her voice was puzzled. She spread her hands, and she and Cass looked at them solemnly for a moment before they exploded into laughter, for Lisa's hands were bluish and thin, her nails are bitten down to the quick, and the two middle fingers she used to cram together and suck when she was smaller are both a little twisted now.

'He says they're interesting.'

'Interesting!' Cass hooted. 'We know what Halloran means by interesting. He used to say that about Tom's face!'

They both peered at me as if I were something

unconscious lying behind iron bars, and then the laughing started up again, even louder. They rolled against one another's bodies, weak and breathless. You'd think I had no feelings at all.

'*Interesting!*' Cass howled over and over again. She pretended to mop tears of amusement from her cheeks with the filthy old bath-towel. 'Let's give Halloran a surprise!'

She dug down in the pocket of her jeans and drew out a small glass bottle of startling sun-bright scarlet nail polish. 'Let's make your hands more interesting for him. Let's paint your interesting nails to match his interesting jacket!'

Everyone gets at Halloran about his jacket. It's smocked and full and flowing as well as being sheep-scaring scarlet. You can see it coming a mile off. It must have come out of some old wicker basket full of theatrical costumes. You can't buy jackets like that in the shops. Dad says it makes Halloran look even more of a pansy than he really is, and Mum says 'Ssssh!' and glances round nervously at Cass and me, who sit staring into our mashed potato as if we were half-wits and also stone deaf. Then Mum relaxes and giggles and says again: 'Now, ssshh! You don't *know*, and you shouldn't say things like that about people. Halloran's a very nice young man. I *like* Halloran.'

So do I. I like Halloran. I always have. He wouldn't mind if Lisa turned up with scarlet nails the first day he started painting her hands for a big competition. He wouldn't think anything of it. You can't tease Halloran because he doesn't care about anything at all except painting. But he'd have something in his conservatory to get the stuff off. He'd be very careful and gentle with dozens of white balls of cotton wool, and handcream after.

So I don't know why they bothered at all, or why they thought it was so funny; but Cass painted Lisa's chewed uneven fingernails a violent glaring red with the polish, giggling the whole time, and then Lisa started on Cass's neat oval nails. She shook the bottle energetically, and held it up so I could see the little steel balls inside it making slow runnels down the thick red, against the glass. I'd never noticed that before.

'It's clever, isn't it?' said Lisa, seeing me look.

'Not really.'

I watched as each time she drew the small brush out of the bottle neck and carried it over to

Cass's outstretched hand, the gooey red slid to a fat heavy glob at the end of the bristles and threatened to fall.

'You'll make a mess,' I warned her. And sure enough, she did. Cass moved a finger slightly, to field an ant. The blob of polish fell on the ground, and as they both looked up to giggle together, her elbow tipped the bottle.

'See?'

The gummy blood red was sliding all over the earth.

'Grump, grump,' Cass said to me. 'What's *up* with you, anyhow?'

I didn't know. I never do. I turned away from them. It just comes over me in hot and irritable waves and leaves me feeling crabby and tired and lonely, and longing to be far out at sea, lying flat on a rough, wet, sun-shrivelled board with everyone dead in the world except me. The feeling might fade away then.

I want to touch Lisa, so some of it's that. I want to reach my hand out and touch the freckles on her face and know what her fluffy brown hair feels like under my fingers. I want to call her Lissie, like Dad does but Jamieson doesn't; but

Cass would just laugh. I want to know what her skin's like. Once she put both her hands over my eyes when I was fighting Cass to get my share of peanuts back, and I can still remember the soft warm soapy smell of her arms and the feel of her wrists when I reached up to tear her fingers away.

I'd have to pretend I was kissing her arm, I suppose. But I'd be making it all damp and warm again, really, to find that skin soapiness over again, if she'd let me.

I lay beside them, blinking bright coloured watery sun patterns at the streaks of light that poured down between the leaves, thinking, thinking. And as the hours passed, Cass rolled from between the sleeping Lisa and me, and over and over, back into prickly grasses, further and further away, in search of the slipping sunlight. I could hear Lisa's fingers scrabbling the flattened grasses, and a patch of skin on her back where her blouse fell away rose and fell very slightly with every breath.

When Cass was far enough away from us, I stood up and stared into the river, and then turned and woke Lisa.

She sat up, surprised. As soon as I put my

finger on my lips, she looked around to see where Cass had got to. I didn't like that. I knew she was making sure that Cass was still near by, and not, as I myself had been making sure all the afternoon, far enough away.

She clasped her knees and stared at her feet. She wasn't being helpful. I looked at the streaks of mud on her wrists and the horrid red at the end of her bitten fingernails. I couldn't look at her skin. I bent down in front of her, on my heels, and hoped she'd look up.

Cass would have shot out a hand, unable to resist, and toppled me backwards, yelling, into the river. Lisa, too, poked me in the stomach, but gently. I felt it a very long while.

I put my hand out a little, so she would touch it, maybe. But if she didn't I might just have moved it for balance.

'What kept you?' I asked. 'Did you have lots of jobs? You were very late coming today.'

'Nothing kept me,' she said. 'I just came late.'

She's very secretive. She has to be, living with Jamieson. There are so many things that she's been taunted about already at school, she knows not to draw more fire by mentioning that the electricity may be cut off any day, or that those stains on her new French book came from a steady leak through her bedroom ceiling, or that the social worker who's called in quite often since the day her mother ran off, turned up again yesterday. She doesn't even tell Cass about some of the things that happen. I put them together from little things she says, and what I overhear at home, and spiteful whispers behind me on the Fretley bus.

It was mean of me to push her. 'You must have been doing something.'

'Not really, Tom. Please!'

'You must have been.'

'No, I *wasn't.*'

'Of *course* you were doing something, Lisa. If you weren't doing anything, you'd have come, wouldn't you? So what *was* it?'

I was furious with her. She'd taken half the day to come, and when she finally did, it was only to brag that because of this sitting for Halloran, she wouldn't be with Cass and me as much any more. She hadn't even tried to sound sorry about it.

'Go *away*, Tom. Lay *off*. You don't own me. I'll come just as late as I like!'

I stood up at once and started pacing up and down the river bank.

'Grump, grump,' she teased me from where she sat, cross-legged, in the grass. 'Grump, grump. Grump, grump.'

I realized I must be looking exactly like my dad to her. He paces when he's angry, and she and Cass used to tease him about it, too, by tagging along behind him and getting under his feet deliberately whenever he turned.

I could have let it go then, stopped my scowling, and smiled. I wish I had. But suddenly – and I don't understand what made me do this, really I don't, and I feel awful about it – I changed the pacing like my father into her own father's slow and creepy slouch, into the imitation of Jamieson that Cass and I have practised for years, hidden away out of sight in the ice house, but never ever showed Lisa.

I did all the horrid bits, too, like the way that he picks at the muck on his jacket, and grins and looks sideways whenever he says things he thinks might upset you, and pokes in the right ear with one of his fingers and then looks to see what he's found.

And right through I kept up a low fierce whisper that wouldn't wake Cass but which Lisa could hear and she couldn't mistake – her father's hoarse growl which I've worked on and worked on, and I was so proud of before.

'Have you got that job done, Lisa? About time, too, girl. But don't you rush off. Before you goes haring around behind the ice house with that hellion Cass and her half-wit twin brother, there's plenty more things you can do here at home.'

I ticked them off on my fingers, just the way he would. I could half-feel her staring at me, open-mouthed, but I carried on.

'First, you can water the carrots. I know it's been pouring with rain all the morning, but you can't never be too sure. And then you can brush the cobwebs out of that rabbit hutch I wouldn't let you get no rabbit for, in case it snuck out and chewed up my lettuces. Next you can rearrange my poisons, my girl, in order of how long they take to kill, and how much it hurts. And polish all those steel breakback traps till they shine, would you, Lisa? As soon as you've done that little lot, you can tidy up the compost heap as it's got in a bit of a mess what with throwing things on it. And, Lisa, before you go off—'

I only realized when I heard her sob. I'd have stopped myself sooner if only I'd known. At least, I tell myself I would, but then, why ever did I start? Was it simply to see if I matter to her? If I can't make her cry, then I can't make her smile. Was I checking to see I could hurt her before I would give her the chance to hurt me?

But I didn't know she was crying. It wasn't my fault that I went on and on so. You see, I never look at Lisa's face. I haven't for ages. I can't. So I look at her knees or ankles or hands, and sometimes I watch the side of her head when she's busily talking to Cass and won't notice. But never her face or her eyes any more, except in the grimy bus window. I can't, in case she should see me.

So I didn't know that her cheeks were streaming with tears and her shoulders were shaking until she made that awful noise in her throat. I'm so stupid I hate myself sometimes. I stopped and said I was sorry at once. But she jumped to her feet, and shaking her head at me wildly, she reached out to slap the side of my face as hard as she could.

I ducked so she'd miss. I couldn't stop myself. She lost her balance and fell, and cut her knee so it started slowly beading with blood. And it was then that my stomach first seized up with this cramp that comes back and comes back.

I reached out to lift her up.

'Lisa,' I said. 'Lissie!'

She snatched her hand away from mine as if I'd scorched her. She ran off between the trees of the spinney, and round behind the ice house towards the footpath that leads to her home.

She never came back. And I haven't seen her since, not once, and now Jamieson says that I won't, the whole summer. He says that she's gone.

Chapter 4

I waited for her all yesterday. I was sure she'd come. I gave Cass the slip as soon as breakfast was over and hurried down here alone, and hung around beside the river, waiting for Lisa to finish sitting for Halloran and come and find me. I had no food and nothing to read, I'd left the house in such a rush, but I couldn't settle down on the bank in case the long grass hid me from Lisa when she arrived, and thinking I hadn't even bothered to come, she turned back again without my having heard her.

I waited all day. I plaited grass stalks endlessly. I tormented ants and every other earthbound crawler I saw with obstacles I scoured the bank and spinney to find. I tried to whistle my way through all the songs and hymns I've ever been forced to learn, though in the end it was the whistling itself and not, as it is usually, the tunes that I found defeating me.

She didn't come, though I started up over and over again, thinking I heard the gentle steady rustle she makes as she picks her way through the spinney. I carried on waiting although I was painfully hungry. I kept on waiting even after I knew she couldn't come, it was far too late.

I was still looking up hopefully when Halloran himself came crashing unmistakably through the thick undergrowth, swinging the canvas bag he carries his painting stuff round in against every tree trunk he passed, yelping and cursing at each lurking clump of stinging nettles that got at him through his thin socks, and wailing as he unhooked the smocking on his precious jacket from bramble after bramble. (Dad says Halloran could frighten a tractor the way he walks over our land.)

As soon as he recovered from the shock I gave him scrambling to my feet, he started attacking me. 'What are you *doing* here? It's *terribly* late. It's past ten o'clock! You should have been home for supper *hours* ago. You're usually up in your *bedroom* by now. There's going to be an awful, *awful* row when you get back!'

He was quite right. There was, and I had known it all the time. It was just that, until I heard Halloran's vivid prophecy, it hadn't seemed to matter. But now I obediently picked up my sweater and shambled off, too miserable even to speak, far too preoccupied to wonder what on earth Halloran was doing prowling around down behind the ice house in the strange summer half-dark.

It was nearly half past when I walked through the kitchen door and into the 'awful, *awful* row' that Halloran had predicted. There was the usual horrible crop for The List: *thoughtless* and *inconsiderate*, *becoming-very-unreliable-these-days* and *difficult-to-live-with*. Mum even added on *late bloomer*, reminding Dad as he strode furiously up and down the kitchen that they were lucky in a way, Cass had been *difficult-to-live-with* for months. Maybe she meant it, deep down, as a kind of consolation to me; but, if she did, it didn't work very well. I've never liked comparisons between me and Cass. I've come off worse too often. And after they'd sent me to bed

I lay awake for hours and hours, smarting from what they'd said and, worse, how they'd said it.

I tried to comfort myself by watching the sort of shimmering night wall shadows that Cass used to tease me about whenever I was upset at nights. 'That one looks just like a kitten,' she'd say. 'Really it does, Tom. Look! Well, then, look a bit harder! That bit at the top of the door is its *ear*.'

She would keep on and on at me until in sheer self-defence I tore myself away from my fretting and tried to see the kitten on the wall. At last it would be there, poised watching me, fat and perfect, and buffing its whiskers with one of its paws.

'I see it!' I would call out excitedly. 'That line down the wall is its back, isn't it? And that dark patch just there is the end of its tail curled behind, right?'

I'd look round at Cass, who hadn't answered. She would be stuffing her face in her pillow in glee, for she'd caught me again the very same way she always did. And when I looked back at the wall again, the kitten was gone.

I'm not there beside her to be teased any more. One day Dad hauled my bed along the passage and into the cold, oddly shaped little room at the end that he'd been using as an office. He moved his office stuff out bit by bit, his files and notebooks and endless cardboard boxes stuffed with receipts, and put them in the only attic room that has a light. And ever since, whenever he's come down from working out wages or paying the bills, he's been in a temper. He says his brains are so addled from banging his head against the rafters, he's made enough mistakes to go bankrupt twice over and have to sell the farm. He doesn't move my bed back, though.

I knew that if Cass and I had still been together, then under the cover of darkness and in response to that brutal and persistent questioning that she starts up the moment she senses that something has happened, I would have told her why I was so late home. I would have told her about the dreadful quarrel with Lisa, and how she ran off.

Cass would, I know, have promised there and then that just as soon as we woke up she'd go with me down to Jamieson's cottage and smooth things over for me. She would have come, in spite of the seagull and not having been down that footpath for years. She's always helped me before when things have needed explaining. She knows she explains things far, far better than I ever can.

Cass always helps, in one way or another, even when she doesn't mean to. She's never the least bit horrified by any of the horrifying things I have to steel myself to tell her. She usually thinks they're funny. And so she makes me see, as she sits up in bed, bright-eyed and eager, hoping for worse, that what I'm telling her is not so very horrifying after all. But last night I wanted more from Cass than comfort. I wanted to get her to promise to come. She hadn't quarrelled with Lisa, so Lisa would have to listen to her. Cass would sort things out.

I got out of bed and went into the passage. I didn't put the light on. I never do. I padded along very quietly and turned her doorknob as slowly as possible. If you hurry, it clicks.

The door didn't open. I thought it was stuck. I stood there in my pyjamas like an idiot, pushing against the wood panelling with my shoulder, and swivelling the doorknob around in both directions although I know perfectly well which way to turn it. I slept there for years, after all.

I stood shoving silently at Cass's door for such

a long time. I didn't realize that it was locked against me. I hadn't even known there was a key.

I went back to bed, and tried to think things out once again by myself. I decided that I would walk over to Lisa's early in the morning – not so early I risked running into Jamieson, but not so late that Lisa might have finished her jobs and set off already for Halloran's place. I thought that way I could force her into listening to me. I'd have trapped her, wouldn't I?

I could guess she would turn her face away at first, and fiddle with the frayed leather strap that keeps the two halves of their rotting tumbledown garden gate from falling apart. She fiddled with it all the while Cass was pleading with Jamieson to let the seagull go free, the last time we were down there.

I meant to keep on. I can't remember any more what I planned to say to her, but I know that I meant to keep on till she had to stop being so angry at me because I'd have explained. She'd loop the tattered leather strap back around the gateposts and look up at last. I'd help her to get her jobs done. I'd do them myself while she sat perched up on the fencing and talked to me. And afterwards we would walk together back to the bend in the river where Cass would be lying fast asleep – she seems to spend most of her days sleeping now – and everything would be all right again, the same as before, as if we had never quarrelled.

I'd take lots of cherries with me. Lisa loves cherries. Dad tells her she's almost as bad as a finch, the way she gets through his cherries. He sticks out his arms like a scarecrow and flaps at her madly, or crackles lengths of Mum's precious tinfoil in front of her face, till she can't stuff any more in her mouth from laughing, and starts to swallow the stones by mistake. I'd get the cherries out of the large china bowl in the larder before Cass could come down and warn me that they are the only thing you can't make a Granny Pudding without, or anything else that would force me to put them all back. I'd even put them in a new plastic bag, and not just one of the rinsed ones. I'd hide them behind all the Wellington boots till the very last moment before I was ready to leave. I had it all planned.

I still couldn't sleep. I was so anxious I might, just this once, miss the short jarring shudder the yard door makes when Dad pulls it over the tiles to let himself out and join Jamieson doing the milking. It might be morning for him, but for me it's a night noise, like Mum tipping all of the cats out or Dad riddling ashes down inside the Aga, or that eerie train that goes whistling through Fretley. I can wake up for it if I decide to the evening before.

I thought I heard it once, I was so on edge. Then something that sounded like the stifled end of a giggle. It could have been one of the cats. I thought I heard a door closing downstairs almost silently, and then a tiny clattering in the hall. Only a few moments later I was wide awake straining to hear again, thinking I heard odd footfalls in the lane outside. I realized then that I was as strung as a rabbit away from its fences and listening so hard that at any moment I would start thinking I heard the cows breathing away in the barns.

I rolled over onto my stomach and burrowed myself deep down secretly, and thought of Lisa's pale thin fingers as they made that soft scrabbling sound across the dried grasses, and the way that her blouse fell away where she hadn't thought to tuck it in before she fell asleep by my side. The rushes of blood and the rushes of noise inside my burning ears wiped out at last the old night fear I have that every slight creak my old wooden bed makes as I move in it wakes the whole house. And in the end I fell so deeply asleep that I never heard Dad leaving in the morning at all.

I woke up early enough, even so. Dad's toast crumbs lay scattered all over the floor around the draining board where he stands when he's just gazing out, watching weather. His pot of tea was sitting on the table, half-empty and already luke-warm; but when I looked out I saw that the sun was not yet over the sheds and the yard was still in shadow. Lisa couldn't have left for Halloran's yet.

I took all the cherries, the whole lot, a huge fat bagful. Although Dad had left the door unlatched, I didn't go out across the yard. I went out the front door instead. I don't use it much, but it's quieter.

There is a coiled-up early-morning feeling, as if everything around is ready to burst just as soon as a few more people get outside to watch, but right now it's all there, ready and waiting, waiting for then. I'd meant to creep along the side of the hedge, in case Dad noticed from wherever he was working that I was already up and out, and called me over to help lift the other end of this length of wood for him for a moment, or hold that door steady right there till he'd forced a new wedge in to hold it fast, or anything else that would keep me.

I did creep as far as the barn. But on the other side the sun had flooded over, and the steep slope that runs down to the fields looked so long and wide, and the ground after two weeks without any rain was so hard and rutted that I could feel every thin ridge in the earth on the soles of my feet through my shoes. And when I started running, the sharp morning sunlight shone full in my face, dazzling me with its glistening bright silver spangles. I spun the bag of cherries around and around in giant red glittering circles; and all the hummocks I use as footholds for my most enormous high leaps over molehills and thistles and clumps of dried grasses were solid and perfect, and running's the one thing I've always done far, far better than Cass.

I yelled and whooped and baited the whole

run down, as I always used to do when she was there and fell back yards behind me, as she always did. And I slid down into the ditch at the bottom with just the same grin of exhaustion and pride that I used to turn on her to make her get angry, and add to the wonderful, glorious feeling of triumph that beating Cass has always given me.

I lay flat on my back, arms outflung, in the cool, wet-leaved shadowy dip. My whole body felt like a pumping machine. When I closed my eyes I could hear every bit of me going: burstings and thumpings and whirrings and thuddings all over. I lay still and listened to myself slow up again, till everything inside me was settled and quiet enough for me to hear at last the light tattered flags of sound that had been fluttering down from way up on top of the hill where Dad was standing, calling my name.

I didn't look up. That way he couldn't prove I'd heard him calling. I reached for the bag of cherries and slid sideways under the fence, away from the sprinkles and dabs of the green-silver ditch light and into the dark hiding bushes that line the old footpath to Jamieson's house.

* * *

There are quiet and noisy places outside, and Jamieson's footpath was quiet. I had the feeling the song I was whistling was carrying for miles through the still hanging air and warning Lisa of my approach, and after a while I fell silent as well. I hurried on, through unlit green tunnels of hedges and creepers that had cat's cradled overhead a long enough time ago to have discouraged with dark weedy twilight the cheerful bright wild flowers you'd see along any other footpath round here. Or maybe it was Jamieson who frightened them off with his droppings of bran and metaldehyde slug-bait, a sickening overgrown Hansel trailing his pebbles of death through the woods.

I came upon him without warning. I walked round a sharp bend between two enormous sprawled hawthorns to find I was already in the clearing in front of his garden. I'd had no idea the footpath might be coming to an end. I've always remembered the way to his cottage as being far, far longer.

He was stooping over one of his fruit bushes, watching a soft fleshy colourful caterpillar looping its way to the end of a leaf. The spray gun that he was about to turn onto the bush was in his hand at the ready, but Jamieson was quietly watching the caterpillar's last unspoiled busy moments of life before he moved in.

I was much too astonished at seeing him there to watch what I said.

'Why aren't you over at the farm?' I burst out.

It was a bad start. He swivelled round. From inspecting the caterpillar crawling over his fruit bush, he took to inspecting me instead. Cass would have known how to backtrack, how to unsay somehow what she'd just said, or how she'd said it. I didn't. I stood there tongue-tied, fiddling stupidly with that worn leather strap on his gate.

'You don't own me,' snarled Jamieson. 'Yet . . .'

Flushing, I dropped the strap and stared at him. I don't think it ever occurred to me before then that, whenever dry rot was found in the barns, or the price of feed doubled and Dad made his regular all-purpose joke: 'Never mind. The whole lot will be Tom and Cass's problem soon,' all Jamieson's feelings were black ones. I've always imagined myself simply paying him off and watching him pick up his vile equipment and leaving our land for ever. It's never occurred to me to wonder what Jamieson would do or where he would go. But he's worked on this farm for the whole of his life. He was born here, like we were, Mum told me.

'You'd best get back,' he said to me sharply, after a while. 'No point in your hanging round here.'

He went back to watching the caterpillar. I took the opportunity of his back being turned to scramble in between the two halves of gate and come up behind him.

'Lisa! Where's Lisa? I want to talk to her!'

He kept his back to me, deliberately. I could sense he was having to force himself not to turn round. His whole body stiffened.

'I reckon you've done enough of talking to my girl to last both of you a little while.' He twisted the handle of his spray gun round and round. 'You go on home, there's a good lad.'

He made me feel ten years old. I hated him for it. I stepped up and tugged at his greasy jacket sleeve with such force that he had to straighten up to keep his balance, and only then did he turn round and face me again. He had to tip his head back a little to glare at me, we were so close.

I hadn't realized, till he did that, how much I'd grown.

The anger in his voice astonished me. 'You upset my girl,' he hissed. 'You upset my Lisa so much she cried half the night. I don't know what you said to her, or what you did, young Tom. Lisa won't tell. But God help you if I ever find out, because if it's half as bad as I suspect it is, then I'll give you such a hiding as you won't forget in a hurry, your dad's son or not.'

I tried to answer him, to defend myself, to explain. I couldn't. How could I? The horrible pain started up like an adder inside me uncoiling from sleep, and when I tried to look away from Jamieson, to escape from the bitter glittering in his eyes, a pale sickly light lay on everything round me, the garden, his cottage, the trees on all sides, and they swung at me till I was sure I'd be sick there and then on his grass.

'I have to talk to her,' I pleaded. 'Let me see Lisa.'

'No! I won't have it! You've upset her enough! And don't you come sneaking back here again, either. You won't get to see her. She's going away. She's off to her Aunt Bridget in Lincoln this morning, and I'm not coming over to the farm till that bus has pulled out of Fretley with my Lisa on it!'

'She can't! She mustn't!' I fished about desperately. 'What about Halloran?' I thought quickly. 'He needs her, too!'

'Damn Halloran! *Damn* him! *Damn* him!'

He hurled the spray gun down with such force that the handle jammed in and it lay leaking small crystal driblets into the ground. He looked close to tears and worn out, like an old lonely man, and I've never felt sorry for Jamieson before, never.

'He'll just have to make do without her,' he said quietly. 'I'll have to, won't I?'

I reached down to pick up the spray gun before it oozed awful things into the roots of his plants. I handed it back to him without a word.

'That's right,' he said, saddened and exhausted after his outburst. 'You get along home. That's best. Your dad will be needing you today with me not there and this rain coming.'

On the other side of his gate, I looked back. He stood there watching me, waiting for me to go, miserable in front of his miserable cottage with its blistered peeling paintwork and cracked slipping roof tiles. The only person in the world he cared about was going away because of what I'd done. He'd said as much.

'Don't send her!'

All of a sudden it seemed very simple. He'd miss her the moment the bus pulled away. He missed her already just thinking about it. He didn't want her to go. Nor did I. Nor did Halloran. We all wanted Lisa to stay.

'Don't send her! I promise I won't upset her again. I'm sorry I did. But please don't send her away. Don't let her go. You know it won't ever happen again.'

Ignoring me, he started sullenly pumping clouds of spray onto his fruit bushes. For once I didn't care. I wouldn't have cared if he'd stuck red-hot pins into each caterpillar in turn, I just wanted Jamieson not to send Lisa away. Patch after patch of the greenery on the bushes darkened and glistened and gathered huge droplets, and clouds of the fine light mist swarmed back all over his body. He was so rattled he was pumping away against a slight breeze.

I climbed onto the middle rung of his rickety gate and shouted at him.

'Don't send her, *please*!'

'She's going away. It's arranged.'

'The whole summer?'

'That's right.'

'But why? *Why?*'

He pumped and pumped, although the spray gun was quite empty now and just making wheezing whistling noises in the air.

'There's no fit company for my girl here,' he said.

'There's Cass,' I argued.

He gave his short sharp bark of a laugh. It's a nasty sound. He pumped away pointlessly at his fruit bushes. His temper was rising. I saw a shadow of fierce beetroot colour creep up above his jacket collar, as far as his ears.

'What's wrong with Cass?' I demanded.

'Go home. Clear off!'

'What's wrong with Cass?'

I shouted it, and it came out in a deep growl that was so much more like his voice than mine that I slid down a rung in surprise and cracked the rotten bar I fell on.

'Get off my gate!' he roared at me. 'Go home! It's not my job to tell you what's what. No, nor tell your mum and dad neither. So you can keep your head in the sand, just like they do, for all she's your own twin sister. But I've seen what I've seen over at Halloran's place, and guessed at the rest. So my girl's spending the summer in Lincoln, out of harm's way!'

'Harm's way?'

'Go home!'

'*Cass?* Over at *Halloran's* place?'

'I'm warning you, Tom. Be off!'

His voice dropped into a real threat, quiet and frightening, and I ran off between the hawthorns before he came after me. The way seemed more like a tunnel than it had before: darker and more stifling, much more overgrown. The crouching roots caught at my feet as I leaped over them, and creepers tore at my clothing. The few small patches of sky I caught sight of were mottled and bruised and waiting for storm, the air a thin damp cloth over my face, out to choke me. The footpath seemed miles long, endless. But I fell against the ash tree on the edge of the spinney at last, panting and doubled over.

The silence that grew as my own rasping breaths slowly quietened matched a strange steady stillness around me. Nothing moved in the spinney. Not even the leaves on the trees were lifting. I've never known the place seem so out of time. I moved towards the ice house. I wanted to think. The feeling of waiting and quiet now seeped into me as it had into the birds and the squirrels. I picked my way over here very slowly and softly, and kept my eyes on where I was treading. So it was not until I was quite close that I saw Halloran's dropped, forgotten jacket.

As I stood staring, its ripped silken lining was lifted by a warm breath of wind. The sudden movement was startling in that vast horrible stillness. It made me jump.

'Harm's way', Jamieson had said about my sister. 'No fit company for my girl! I've seen what I've seen over at Halloran's place and guessed at the rest.'

And all at once I understood. I saw Halloran's bright scandalizing jacket lying like a dare on the ground outside the private secret place I've shared with Cass as long as I can remember. Halloran was hanging around last night when it was far too dark to paint. He knows my family's evening habits as thoroughly as if he shares them. Cass locks her bedroom door at nights, and dozes all day.

As I stood guessing at the rest, like Jamieson, I seemed to hear over again those muffled furtive sounds downstairs, the footfalls in the lane outside, that stifled torn-off end of a giggle I'd thought was the cat.

Cats don't meet in the ice house.

'Damn Halloran!' I whispered the words I'd just heard Jamieson shouting. I was trying them out for myself, now. '*Damn* him! *Damn* him!'

As if I had unsettled them, the leaves started shimmering and shivering again. A perfect gleaming heavy summer raindrop fell on my hand, another in the patch of dried earth at my feet. I watched it spin, a fat mercurial glob gathering dust. And then another, and another, and more on my face, unless I confused them with all my tears, and the thunder split and ripped and banged overhead, dead with the livid flashes of lightning that lit up the spinney so garishly.

I turned and ran, and the only thing I could think was that the cloud-burst would wash all the spray from Jamieson's fruit bushes. I wasn't glad. I didn't even care, and neither did Jamieson. He'd seen the storm coming and known that it would. I just thought it over and over again as I ran, to blot out the rest.

The paths I took were winding streams like ribbons, they were so wet; and by the time I reached the farm, the yard had flooded into a green-silver lake beneath the huge eerie storm light and I was soaked through to the skin and so chilled, so chilled, I just couldn't stop myself shaking.

Chapter 5

I'm still shivering now. I should have had the sense to change my clothes before I came back here, for though I've rooted all around the filthy damp floor of the ice house to find every single stump of a candle there is, and I've lit them all round me, I'm still so cold I can hardly keep the egg book flat on my knees for trembling, and this pencil is hurting my fingers, I'm having to grip it so tightly to keep it from sliding all over the page.

I have the key, though. I wasn't quite sure what I was after when I caught myself hesitating outside Cass's door instead of keeping on down the hall to my own. My sandals were squelching those growing dark stains into Mum's polished floor, and trickles of rainwater from my hair still filled

81

my eyes, slid down my face and neck, and into this sodden clinging shirt. Perhaps when I stopped just outside I was telling myself I should get on the nearest rug as soon as I could. Perhaps I thought I was after a towel. There are always more on Cass's floor than in the airing cupboard. She rubs her hair dry with them and then simply drops them into the clutter.

Whatever I thought when I stopped, the moment her door closed behind me I knew what I wanted. It's here in my hand now. I'm going to bury it deep in the hard-packed black earth down here under the rotting sack floor, where neither Cass nor Halloran will ever think of looking. I have the key to her room.

That will trap her. I don't think even Cass would dare leave the house after dark if she knew any one of us might tap, tap, tap on her door and then walk right in to find her bedcovers carelessly tossed back, and she herself gone. So there'll be no more little meetings round behind the ice house at nights, or over at Halloran's place, where Jamieson saw what he saw. Cass will never dare risk it. Suppose she were caught? Oh, she could spin her endless sticky word webs the morning after, and flounce: 'Of course I heard you knocking on my door last night! But I just didn't feel like talking. Is that a crime?' Or, full of sleepy morning innocence: 'I did have a strange dream of wood being chopped right outside my room. Could that have been when you were trying to wake me?' And if she were irritable from her persistent lack of sleep, we'd hear something surly like: 'Oh, that was *you* banging on my door last night. I'm sorry I didn't bother to answer. You see I thought it was Tom.'

Spin, spin away, Cass. You always have. But there will be no point in it this time, for even you will be helpless for once without this key you found. Whoever stands knocking may simply push open your bedroom door, and looking around as I did just now, see you aren't there.

Her room has changed, just as it changed once before when I was moved out and Cass just stuffed everything that belonged to me into cardboard boxes and dumped them outside on the landing. The comics fell apart, all out of order; my tapes and CDs were all over the place, out of their boxes and sleeves; and she didn't even bother to make sure the lids were down tight on my oil-paint tins before she tossed them into the boxes: the dark green leaked and ruined both my sheep skulls. And she threw out my model sailing ships. She'd always said before how much she liked looking at the three of them, there on the sill, as if they were sweeping over the fields you can see from the window. But she just piled them up outside in the hall with the rest of my stuff, so that when I walked round the turn at the top of the stairs I snapped off a mainmast she'd left sticking up unprotected.

She wasn't even sorry. I went in with the model in my arms to show her what she'd done, but she didn't even bother to look down from where she was balancing in her socks on the top of the bookcase.

'The tape, Tom,' she said. 'Pass the tape. Is he straight? Have I got him quite straight?'

I looked up and met the huge looming eyes of the beautiful coal-shiny stallion up on the poster that she was struggling to keep flat and straight, spread-eagled against the wall. Sighing, I laid the model sailing ship I spent so many hours making gently down at the end of her bed. There wasn't room for it any longer on the window sill, because she'd already cluttered over my half with her simpering coloured glass squirrels and plastic ponies and fat woolly pom-pom pets with their silly red felt smiles round to their ears and black beady eyes.

Stepping back I said, 'Down on the window side, Cass.' And I felt a bit sorry for him, really, so strong and glossy and doomed to gather dust and fade on the wall looking down on glass squirrels and pom-poms. She could only have taped the two top corners, for it seemed no more than a moment before she took me completely by surprise with: 'Mind, Tom. I'm coming down.'

'Mind *yourself*, Cass!' I howled. But it was too late. She'd already landed with both feet through the sailing ship's poop deck. And though she helped me pick every last minute fragile splinter of wood from her thick woollen counterpane, and I have kept the bits safely in a shoe box, I've never tried to fix the model again.

That stallion isn't on her wall any more. I don't know what happened to him. All the posters are new ones now and they're faces, faces and bodies. They're all real people, and though I don't remember who some of them are, I know I've seen them before. The squirrels and pom-poms and plastic ponies have disappeared, too. She keeps little tubes and pots and bottles and oddly shaped brushes all over the dresser now, though I've never seen her wearing half the colours in the ones I unscrewed on her eyelids, or smelled any of those strange musky smells on her body.

It's one of the things she locks her door for, perhaps.

Her bookcases are stuffed full of shiny magazines with pictures of girls just like her on the front. The covers are so glossy and slippery that they all slithered out across the floor when I just opened one a little. I had to shove them all back. I hope she won't notice I touched them. She has several cartoon books of cats in her bookcase. I didn't know that Cass cared for cats. I can't remember when she last spoke to ours.

But almost everything in her room is new to me. A good half of that rising tide of clutter across her floor that Mum goes on about is made up of clothes I've never seen Cass wearing. There are drawings of dream-like, fantastical countrysides scattered about and pinned to the walls, and notebooks she's coated with vivid swirling patterns in felt-pen colours of all the letters in her name: Cassandra – Cassandra – Cassandra in greens and violets and blues, and oranges, yellows and rich blood reds. Each letter must have taken her hours. No wonder her homework gets worse and worse.

I even found several letters lying about, sent by girlfriends at school she won't get to see all the summer. Nobody ever wrote a letter to me because we'd be separated for forty-two days. In fact I'm not sure I've ever received a letter at all, except from the Fretley library. One of the envelopes is stained with a big brown ring from some half-drunk mug of coffee she's carelessly put down on it. I'd never think of bringing a mug of coffee upstairs, never.

Her room smells funny, like shops at Christmas. My room smells of glue. And scattered all over, lying on sills and the table and bookcases, propped against walls and hanging out of half-open drawers, suspended from lampshades and doorknobs, all over everything are pretty things. Things that catch at the light, small glowing flowery things, dozens of them, just like treasure. Earrings and bangles and slim golden lipstick covers; little enamelled boxes; rings and glass beads; a bright woven watchstrap and two patterned saucers heaped with foreign coins; gleaming glass bottles and jars and small china pots with beautiful labels; bookmarks and picture postcards, delicate grey dried flowers and tightly rolled balls of multi-coloured wool. There's even a mobile hanging over her bed, eight small silver dolphins forever swimming through air. Just looking around, you'd think a jackdaw lived here, really you would.

Where has all this stuff come from? Where does she get the money to pay for it all? Does she steal it? Or are these presents, presents from Halloran? And why haven't Dad and Mum noticed?

I moved towards the dresser and slid out the stiff shallow drawer we once partitioned with cardboard to keep our two sets of marbles from rolling together. She's thrown the cardboard partition away. There's a nest of silly pretty bright-coloured underwear in there now, things I didn't even know that she wore.

I didn't want to touch them but I knew the key was in there somewhere. I know Cass, you see. And so it was, right at the very back, hidden well away where no one would ever think of looking, in one of those slim silver tubes the girls giggle over and lend to one another in lunch break when they think the boys are not looking. The silky soft materials brushed at the hairs on my skin as I drew out my hand, and just for a moment elastic tangled my fingers. Do they all wear stuff like this under their plain old school blouses? Does Mum pass on things like this to Lisa as well?

I slammed the drawer shut and was about to make for the door when I caught sight of myself in the mirror. I looked so furtive, like Jamieson stalking something behind a hedge, that it made me stop and think; but though I opened my hand and stared at the key for a moment, I didn't put it back again in the drawer. I closed my fingers around it more tightly.

I hate looking into mirrors. I always have. When I was small I used to think for a moment it was Cass standing there, set-faced and grave. I'd wonder why she wasn't smiling at me. I don't make that mistake any more. We haven't looked anything like one another for years. You'd never guess we used to be twins. But I still don't like mirrors. Cass does. She spends her whole life looking into them. I don't know how she can. I look at myself looking back like that, a quiet foreigner with still grey eyes, and I want to shiver. I have that look that Halloran complained about whenever he tried to paint me. He said I was too well tucked away. He's right. I'm so well tucked away that, for all they know, I'm not in here at all. No wonder he chose me to be his Sad Scarecrow. To tell the truth, I'm not sure I would recognize my face in a crowd.

'Boo!' I said softly to the reflection.

My voice came out a little gruffly again, as it had when I shouted at Jamieson. The grey-eyed foreigner stared back, unmoved; but his hand closed as tightly around the key as my own, his knuckles whitened too.

I'd better bury it. The last two candle ends are guttering now. The others have all spluttered out and I am colder than ever. I'll check on Cass every night from now on, more than once. I'll keep awake, listening. I'll watch the front lane from my window. And if I find she's slipped out anyway, I'll follow her.

After all, unlike her, I'm in practice.

Chapter 6

I never thought to bring more candles down here today. To find the egg book, I've had to scrabble about on my knees in the blackness with all the rich fat drip, drip, drippings echoing around me to sound like something giving way at last after hundreds of years. And only here, curled up against the dank wet tunnel brickwork, where what green and watery daylight there is still reaches in, can I see to write in the next seven things on The List, the last nasty harvest, all mine this time, all things about me.

Tom Fool, a stone, deaf, stupid or deceitful. There. There's the first five. I've written them down very neatly, under *late bloomer*. I'd not forgotten any, though it's been more than a week now since that great thunderstorm, since I sneaked back sodden wet from burying Cass's key in the ice house and ran straight into Dad, who was black with mud, drenched and furiously angry.

'Where have you *been* all this time? Where *were* you?' He shook me, hard. 'Any other Tom Fool would have seen this storm coming and *known* there'd be extra work for us all! Why on earth couldn't *you*?' He hurled my wet-weather boots in my face, shoved Jamieson's heavy spade in my hand, and half pushed, half kicked me out of the kitchen across the swimming yard to the very same slope I'd only that morning leaped down like a mad jumping bean.

He stopped in the low meadow, where two blocked drainage ditches were making a rising swamp of the crops the other side of the fence. The sight of it riled him all over again.

'Why didn't you come back this morning?' he bellowed at me through the rain. 'You knew I needed you! A *stone* would have heard me calling from the top of the hill! Now *dig*, Tom! *Dig!*' And in between his own immediate strong savage cuts of the spade into tangles of weeds and swept mud that were blocking the easy flow of the water,

I heard him shouting: 'You're either *deaf*, *stupid* or *deceitful*, Tom. You take your pick!'

Tom Fool, a stone, deaf, stupid or deceitful. I dug to them with Jamieson's unwieldy spade. I whispered them over and over to myself as I worked, like a charm to keep myself going. I even made up a little private tune for them, to whistle whenever Dad was working too closely beside me. I dug and dug with the sound of them smarting away in my brain, *Tom Fool, a stone, deaf, stupid or deceitful*, again and again.

The rain went on and on and on. I've never felt so wet in my life. I was aching with cold and tiredness and hunger before we began, but after a short while of digging away at that sodden clogged ditch, each muscle was shrieking, my arms felt red hot in their sockets.

I wouldn't give up. The more it hurt, the harder I cut at that choked reedy mess, as if the pains weren't in my back and neck and shoulders and arms, but in each spadeful of the matted black earth I prised up and hurled to the side, out of the way.

Soon, at least, I wasn't cold any more. I was sweating and glad of the sharp washing rain. And gradually, too, my body gave in and went with the binding rhythm of the digging; and though every bit of me still ached and ached, I dug my way steadily through the grey cloud-swamped light after Dad till together we'd cleared and widened the whole way along the low meadow, and all the gathered banked-up rainwater that had been flooding down the steep slope could funnel into the main ditch at last, and spin and eddy easily down to the rising river.

We could have stopped then. The other ditch didn't matter so much. The rain was slackening, and it was still draining, if slowly. But I moved in front of Dad, who was taking a break leaning over his spade, and shaking my dripping bothersome hair from my eyes, I started digging along that ditch too, without saying a word.

He didn't speak either. He just sighed, uprooted his spade and fell in behind me. There was a funny twisted grin on his face, but I ignored that. Working in front is much harder: you are the one to break up the earth which the second man simply clears out to the sides. I hadn't realized that before. Dad knew, but he never offered to change places again. From time to time he glanced at me out of the corner of his eye, but I pretended

I hadn't noticed. I knew he was waiting for me to admit to myself I was beaten, to step back and rest on my spade for a while, just as he had, and afterwards fall in behind him again.

I wouldn't do it. I wouldn't stop. I wouldn't even slow the pace he'd set when he was so very angry before. I kept on stubbornly, though I knew how much stronger he was, and how he could keep working as long as he wanted. The muscles in my arms felt like burning steel wires, close to snapping. From time to time, I saw stars. Each spadeful weighed half a ton, the earth was so sodden and weedbound. Clearing a drainage ditch on a farm like ours is not like digging a flower garden, you know.

If he'd said: 'Do you want to call it a day, Tom?' I would have ignored him. He knew that and left me alone. He just kept digging a couple of paces behind me with that odd sideways grin on his face, even after both ditches were draining better than they have in years. He was still grinning when I'd kept on so long that the beading of sweat across his forehead had turned to a clammy grey sheen all over his face. The grin looked a little strained then, though.

God knows what I looked like under my coating of black splattered ditch mud. I've never felt so tired in my life, but I kept going and going until, at last, he cracked and shouted: 'Whoah, there, Tom boy! Let's go on up. I'm famished!'

I gave one last mighty swing of the spade. It nearly killed me. I don't know how I even lifted my arms, but I did, and the huge heavy lump of wet earth soared up and over behind me and barely missed hitting him good and hard on the shoulder. Then I grinned too, just as if he were Cass, beaten hollow for ever and ever.

'All right, lad,' he said. 'Don't go mad!' But I could tell he was pleased. I could tell from his voice. I could tell from the look on his face.

It's been like that all week. I've kept up with him, job for job, and he knows it too. So does Mum. She puts my plate down along with Dad's and Jamieson's now, instead of after. She gives me full helpings like them: double-yolked eggs, large chops and whole quarters of pie, and she's stopped asking me if I've picked up a cold every time that my 'Thanks, Mum' comes out gruff.

And Dad says 'What do you think?' to me now as well as to Jamieson. 'Slate that shed while the rain's still off? What do you think, Tom?'

Jamieson sits hunched over his food, forlorn, in disgrace. He doesn't snatch at the bread rolls any more, he's so cast down. And he won't even look at Cass, let alone sit opposite her, he's missing his Lisa so badly.

Mum sniffs the air suspiciously when he goes out. She guessed that he was drinking three days before we found his empty bottles under the hedge. So it was me Dad sent on the roof to patch up that leak, and me who's been out on the tractor all week. I'd never worked with the tractor before though I'd driven it back to the farm at night often enough. I managed pretty well for a starter, Dad said. At least I haven't lost any limbs, which is more than poor Jamieson would have managed, the state he's been in. Dad's furious with him. 'He's not fit to feed chickens,' I over-heard him saying to Mum. 'Thank God I've got Tom now, that's all I can say.'

'Remorse,' Cass explained after Jamieson staggered perceptibly crossing the kitchen on his way home last night after supper. 'It's remorse.

He's sorry he poisoned his Lisa now. He misses her almost as much as Tom does.'

Though Dad's immediate 'Stop that!' was directed at Cass, it wasn't her that he and Mum were looking at so very sharply across the table, and I went red in spite of myself. I felt like killing Cass. She's been like that all week, full of sly silly hints about Lisa and me, and giggles and teases, as if she hasn't even noticed I've stolen her bedroom-door key and spoiled her own game for good.

I haven't got to watch her once, either. I've planned to every evening, but though I go up to bed very early, the first thing I know is Dad shaking my shoulders at dawn, waking me for the milking that Jamieson hasn't once arrived in time for this week.

That's why I planned to go to Halloran's this morning. When Dad said: 'Take a day off, Tom. You've earned it,' I thought at once of walking over there to see what was to be seen and guess at the rest just like Jamieson did, and check on my sly cunning giggling sister once and for all.

She really didn't want me to go. When she walked in and heard me suggesting to Mum I go and winkle some of the egg money Halloran owes out of him, she panicked.

'I'll go. I don't mind going.' She glared at me. 'Let Tom stay home. He's worked all week. He needs a good rest. I'll take the egg bill over myself. I could do with a walk.'

'I'm going, Cass,' I told her.

I'm not sure how I sound different to everyone now, but I know that I do. Although Cass frowned, Mum didn't even wait for the usual wrangling to start. She simply handed Halloran's egg bill over to me.

'All sorts of things are changing round here,' Dad said to no one in particular as he and Mum left the room.

The moment the door closed Cass sprang on me like the tiger she is when she's thwarted, and snatched the egg bill out of my hand.

'I'm warning you, Tom. If you come crawling over to Halloran's place, spying on me, you'll be sorry! I'm not the only one with secrets round here, and I'll pay you back!'

I wasn't going to argue. I'd told her I was going, and with or without the egg bill, I was going to go. So I made for the door.

'You're growing just like him!' she taunted. 'With all your spying and trapping and spoiling things. You're turning into a right little Jamieson!'

I banged the door as hard as I could, and broke into a run across the yard to get away. But I still heard her shrill voice jeering at me through the wide open kitchen window.

'You want to watch yourself, you know. You're halfway there already, you nasty, nasty, creeping, peeping Tom!'

A right little Jamieson. Creeping, peeping Tom. I ran straight down here to write the two of them down and stop them spinning around in my head; but now I can't do it, they're just so horrible. I can't write them in. I can't. I've never had to put anything from Cass down before, and I know if I do they will shriek out at me from the drab closely written pages of the egg book as if they were written in glitter, or blood, or something. I'll never get them out of my head.

So I've got to get Cass to take them both back. I've got to make her say they're not true. I'm going to go and find her right now, even if it means following her over to Halloran's place and risking her terrible temper. I'll take her the key back to prove that I'm sorry. I'll make her say they're not true, the things that she said. She'll take them back, I know she will. She's my sister.

Chapter 7

I walked the long way over the fields to Halloran's place, instead of taking the short cut across the old bridge. It's slippy and rotten enough when it's dry; I hate crossing there in bad weather. And I wanted to give Jamieson's cottage a very wide berth. It was over a week since he'd sent Lisa away; but though he'd said nothing more about that to me at the farm while we were working together, I still thought my luck might run out if I ran into him on his own ground. If I'm frank, he was scaring me rather. It was horrible watching him missing her so, and much worse since the morning we found those bottles of his in the hedge.

I missed her too, that's what he didn't know. I thought about Lisa the whole day, and found myself wishing again and again that I'd bitten my tongue on that day at the river. If I'd kept quiet then, instead of traipsing miserably through the thick mud to Halloran's place to tell Cass how sorry I was for stealing her door key and all the rest, I might have been striding down the footpath to Jamieson's cottage to look for Lisa on my first day off work.

She might have quickly shut the door in my face, and left me standing like a clod on her doorstep. She might have laughed in my face. She might have agreed to come for a short walk, but rather unwillingly; and then we would have to walk over the fields, embarrassed and barely speaking, and each time I glimpsed the side of her face as she ducked through a fence, her guarded look might have frightened me into a silence to last the whole way through that field to the next.

She might have smiled, though. I might have dared to smile at her, and she might simply have smiled back at me. She might have slipped out of her house to join me so quickly I'd have to remind her to go back inside for a coat, it was raining so hard. She might have squeezed my hand when I took it, to show me she was glad that I'd come. She might have let me jump her down from the stiles, just like Dad does. I crossed two whole fields working out which walk from her house has most stiles.

We'd be soaked. It was soaking, a really wet walk. You couldn't take a step without sinking and squelching. My shoes had clogged thick and heavy with all the mud. But I plodded on, and talked to Lisa inside my head, and by the time I came to Halloran's place, I felt quite cheerful. I was surprised.

Halloran lives east of Jamieson's cottage, in the small isolated house he grew up in with his Aunt Susan. I love Halloran's house, and all the things in it. I've spent hours there, picking through his huge colourful art books, wrapped up in the folds of Aunt Susan's thick red velvet curtains, while Cass sat, forbidden to speak for the moment, as Halloran prowled round the room, looking at her different ways through the mirrors and rich polished woods, until he was ready to paint her again.

He's always preferred painting Cass. She has a gift for sitting, he says. Where frozen blankness used to sweep over me the moment he reached for a paintbrush, Cass sat as she'd been told, chin up, eyes level, a finger lifted, whatever he'd said, as if she were perfectly living, as if she had just that very moment stopped laughing, or fallen that way unawares.

She sat so well, he even used to let her chatter to him while he worked. He'd never let me. If I so much as cleared my throat, it was:

'Sssh! Up a bit! Can you go back to how you were? Tom, can you look out the *window* again!'

These flurries of irritation never swirled around Cass. She'd sit there, calmly nattering away.

'Smith's farm boy thinks you're really weird, Halloran. I suppose he means living out here, all alone, and not having any proper job, and that horrible jacket you wear all the time.'

'I suppose he does, Cass. I do hope this nice light holds out just a bit longer. We're doing amazingly well here.'

I'd wander off around the house, fingering, fingering. I fiddled with the heavy brass handles on the mahogany sideboards, and traced with my fingertips the pattern whorls on the bookcase. I rubbed the bevelled glass panes of Aunt Susan's china cabinet with my sleeve ends till they threw prisms with the sunlight again. I listed the different woods over and over again to myself as I wandered around: satinwood, harewood, rosewood, pearwood, holly, mahogany, oak.

Soon, when the light had quite gone, I'd hear them packing up in the conservatory, and Cass's faint persistent barrage of criticism for Halloran's day's work.

'I wasn't slouching like that. I *know* I wasn't. Halloran, why have you painted my hair that very nasty mud colour? My arms aren't that long. No one's are. If you wanted to paint a gorilla, why didn't you ask Tom to sit?'

On she would grumble, not even listening to herself, while Halloran calmly wiped off his brushes and screwed the tops back on his jars. He wasn't listening either. I'd settle down behind Halloran's enormous goldfish tank and chase his sluggish overfed pets round and round Aunt Susan's favourite porcelain mermaid, which Halloran dropped in there one afternoon, to amuse them. I sat and waited for Cass's flagging clockwork grouses to run right down.

'Don't meddle,' Halloran would say, as she mixed up his pens and pencils and chalks, and laid his clamps and hammers down where he would take a week to find them again. 'Just put that back where it was, if you would.'

'Oh, please, Cass! No!' he'd cry, seeing her use his best knife to prise off a tin lid. But she was already sniffing at the pale smelly shrinking liquid. Before he could snatch at the tin, she had put it down, sneezing. 'You've slopped it all over my *drawings*!' he'd wail.

She'd give him the slip again and again between the tall easels and stacked-up canvasses, behind all the paintings that leaned back to back. He'd hear the tell-tale snap of his slim brittle sticks of black charcoal, or the noisy cascade of his tacks on the tiles, but by the time he reached her she would already be leafing her way through his library books with her charcoally fingers.

'This one was due back in October!' she'd tell him, with spiteful relish. 'Hey, Halloran! This one is *March*!' She'd torture Halloran, until he would beg us to leave.

'Look, Cass,' he'd plead. 'It's getting *dark*. I'm going out myself, in a moment. Oh, *please*, Cass. Won't you go home now?'

At last, without warning, she'd reach for her coat and make for the door.

'Look at this *mess*!' Halloran would howl after me as I scooted out in her wake. 'Look at this *mess*, Tom!'

He never dared complain directly to Cass. She has a gift for sitting, you see.

It was the same whenever he painted Lisa. Cass flitted to and fro, alternately making distracting faces at Lisa from behind his back, or writhing around on the floor, trying out some strange body position she'd found in the oriental art book he kept high up on a shelf in his bedroom, its spine turned to the wall. Halloran knew very well who was making the noise; but it would always be me, sitting reading in absolute stillness, half-hidden in curtains, he ended up blaming.

'Please stop that awful thumping, Tom! Are you breathing like that to *annoy* me?'

Even after Cass settled to some quiet, un-distracting activity, like dipping his precious pastels one by one into turps, he'd still end up getting ratty with me. Lisa's hard to paint, like I am. She has a tenseness about her that ends up looking like wood on his canvasses. He'd draw her pale set anxious face, crowing with triumph because he was sure that he'd got it this time, and a few sittings later he'd be snapping at me because some half-painted marionette he'd never seen before in his life was staring glassily back from the easel. He only kept painting the two of us every now and again out of pride. He hated doing it really. It had him close to tears of frustration at times. It's just that the only paintings Halloran ever sold were paintings of Lisa or me. People did like the studies he did of Cass, but nobody wanted to buy them.

Cass told him once:

'You know what it is, Halloran? These paintings of me are all *soppy*.'

Halloran went pale, and then turned as red as his jacket. She'd really hit home. You've got to admire her, she knows how to put the boot in, does Cass. She'd just put it well into me, after all.

'*Boots, boots, boots*,' I sang as loudly as I could, through the rain. The marching came out wrong, of course, because of all that field mud squelch-sucking at my shoes so hard, my heels kept slipping halfway out. But I kept at it.

They must have heard me coming a mile off;

and yet when I finally ducked through the sheets of grey rainwater slopping over the edges of Halloran's gutter, and stork-stood in his conservatory doorway to prise my mud-clogged shoes off onto the step, I might have crept the whole way over there in my socks for all the notice anyone took. I'd reckoned on Cass's ignoring me; but I thought Halloran might have shouted hello from the kitchen. I hadn't quarrelled with him, after all.

'Hey, Halloran!' I shouted, peeling my sodden jacket off. 'Halloran!'

Chapter 8

I knew they were in there. The dark mottled blur of Halloran's jacket was shifting here and there on the other side of the frosted-glass door, as he chinked spoons and saucers down on a tea tray. And I could hear from the pantry behind the familiar clatter of every biscuit-tin lid in turn being hopefully prised off in search of stale cake.

I hung my wet jacket over the back of Halloran's easel, and hearing a sudden tell-tale pattering around my feet, swooped to rescue a pile of pencil drawings from all the little drip pools I'd started. They were hands, all of them. Hands. Hands pressed together, hands pointing, hands making finger steeples; hands cupped and pleading and stroking, and hands lying quietly in a lap.

I liked the hands stroking best, and Aunt Susan's ancient velvet tea cosy looked wonderfully curled up and cat-like under the thin roving fingers. I shuffled that one onto the top, and propped the whole lot up against the easel, where he'd already started on hands in a lap, in sad drab rainy-day colours.

I didn't like the painting at all. The hands lay in the skirt, limp and horrid, like newborn kittens on an old cloth. A faint bluish tinge, as if the twisted fingers were cold, was almost the only difference in colour between the hands and the dreary grey lap. Before I even reached for the competition details he'd pinned to the edge to encourage himself, I thought to myself he was wasting his time.

I'd known from what Lisa had told us that this competition was something special. But till I fingered that thick grey parchment brochure, and traced the hard raised royal blue signatures of all those titled sponsors, and saw the lions snarling at one another across the bright coat-of-arms on the front, I hadn't realized just how special it was. And when I opened it, I understood at last why Halloran had been so rash as to promise Lisa four pounds an hour to sit for him, when he's so poor he can't even pay off his egg bill. If Halloran won any of these prizes, he could pay Lisa ten times what she'd earned, and still be in clover for months.

He might not win, though. It would have been a giant gamble, with Jamieson lurking around counting Lisa's hours and pounds up all day. Dad always said that Halloran would stop at nothing to get a sitter, but I thought perhaps it was just as well for him that Lisa had gone off to Lincoln. Especially with that awful painting up on the easel. He was confident, though. I could see that. He'd already filled in the entry form. *Hands in a Lap*, he had written, and underneath, *Girl, Moth and Candle*.

I looked around for that. I hoped for his sake he'd made it a sight more cheerful than *Hands in a Lap*. I couldn't see it anywhere. But to my astonishment, whenever I prised two leaning canvasses apart, or slid out a drawer, or stepped around an easel, wherever I looked there were paintings of Cass. Cass. Nothing but Cass. Here, there and everywhere, whichever way I turned, I was stared at or looked through or smiled on by

Cass. Halloran's conservatory was just as full of paintings of my sister as it always used to be, yet all but a few were quite new to me. I stood there, baffled. It was a while before I realized she'd simply carried on sitting for him all these months, without a word to Mum and Dad – or to me.

Cass is *amazing*. I swivelled round and round, staring. And Halloran's amazing, too. What Cass said when she put the boot in that day must have jolted him out of his rut in a hurry. These paintings of Cass weren't soppy at all. They were marvellous.

There she was on the plant ledge over there. He'd painted her as a bakery serving-girl handing over a bag of buns, the counter edge wedged into her stomach. Her face was afloat with boredom. She took my breath away, really she did. You'd never have guessed from the look on her face that she'd just sneaked out of her bedroom after dark to sit for this painting, and if Dad caught her, he would have torn her apart.

Propped up by the door, she was painted wrapped in one of Aunt Susan's bath towels, her bare foot resting on a rickety wicker seat chair from the kitchen, her face half-hidden by falls of lank, dripping hair. Was this the painting that so shocked Jamieson? Was this what set him off guessing at the rest, deciding my sister was no fit company for his Lisa? I couldn't see it myself. The longer I looked at the painting, the more I liked it. Cass looked so pink and steaming and absorbed in her toes. The line of water beads across the skin of her shoulder looked so round and glassy I stuck out a sudden finger to touch one. I wanted to see if it was still wet.

I found *Girl, Moth and Candle* hidden in a corner, protected by ripped-up squares of old sheeting and turned away with its face to the wall. I swivelled it round and sat with my back against the fishtank, and looked at it.

Cass again. Cass with a candle, this time, a candle end stuck on a dirty cracked saucer. She crouched beside it, cupping its colours and shine with her hands, catching its tossed-out circles of warmth like Jamieson catches at finches. She had the same look on her face as he gets when the exhausted wing fluttering slows up at last, or when some fold in his netting tangles and steadies the tiny thumping body so he can move in. His trapping look: not cruel, that wouldn't be fair; absorbed, rather. Cass looked like that.

She was waiting, quite still, for the moth to come close. She was watching for it to flutter down out of the darkness so she could cup it in her hands before the frail wings singed in the heat from the candle, before she heard that short soft fizz-spit of the moment it flew in the flame. I looked at the vast swirling, dizzy-making way that Halloran had painted the brickwork behind and above her, and felt as if I were beside her again, down in the chill of the ice house.

It was a wonderful painting. I dipped my fingers into the fishtank and watched the only two goldfish that were left heave themselves reluctantly off to the sides.

So that's what they'd been up to. Paintings. Paintings. That's what they were doing round behind the ice house that night. Halloran was lugging his great canvas bag there simply in order to work on a painting of Cass, his best painting ever, a painting he hoped would win him the money and time to paint more. And all my suspicions were nonsense. Cass was quite right. I'd been another Jamieson, with all my nasty creeping and peeping. I'd even stolen her door key.

I felt so tired of myself, and ashamed. I slid my hand down deeper into the water, which stilled again slowly and warped my fingers till they looked all crooked, like Lisa's. The rain rattled steadily down on the skylights above as I sat there, working it out. Cass hadn't told Dad she was still coming over here. But, then again, Dad only stopped her because of his silly squabble with Halloran, last haymaking. And Cass had tried. I heard her again, as clearly as if it were yesterday:

'If Mum can sell eggs to Halloran, why can't I still sit for him. He wants sitters far more than he wants eggs!'

I looked around at all these paintings he'd done of her since and I thought she was right. You couldn't blame her. And if I'd only pitched in with her back then, while she was still trying to argue it out with Dad, between us we might have changed his mind. Things might have worked out differently for us both.

She'd had to manage without me, though. I must have been too busy trailing after Jamieson, or sitting around on the ice-house floor getting all the little details of her daily wrangles with Mum and Dad written neatly down on The List for her. *Stubborn* and *argumentative* I'd copied down, again and again, while she fought it out by herself, and lost.

I'd been no help to her then. So if, now, everything had changed, and she chose to spend her days, her nights even, sitting for Halloran, then it really was none of my business – no more than it was Jamieson's – no more than my days and nights were any longer any business of hers.

And just suppose that my suspicions had turned out right. What of it? Should that make any difference to me? I somehow, sitting there, wasn't sure. I can't be both her brother and her jailor. I have to choose, and face the fact there aren't too many men like Halloran, absorbed so simply in the ways a face and body can be painted. Next time it might be someone else, someone like me. Someone who wants my sister the same way that, if I'm halfway honest with myself, I have to say I want Lisa.

I sat there thinking for a very long while. I never even heard the kitchen door open. And when Halloran came in at last, and saw me stroking the porcelain mermaid's cool creamy skin with my fingertips, he didn't say a word about it. That's Halloran for you. That's why I like him. He just closed the door that little bit more firmly behind him, and came across to stand at my side.

I nodded at the door he'd closed so carefully. 'She's in there, isn't she?'

He didn't answer me at once. He reached across the cluttered ledge for the fish food, and started feeding the last of his fish.

'The one you liked best died,' he said. 'Did Cass tell you?'

'Cass hasn't told me anything for months.'

'Oh. Sorry.'

'I expect you overfed him,' I said.

He put the top back on the fish food at once, and it was when he put the small cardboard tub back onto the ledge that I first saw the tiny gold shimmering painting of my favourite goldfish. Just flecking in the scales alone must have taken him days. He must have kept the fish in the freezer whenever he wasn't working on it.

'Oh, Halloran! How *could* you?'

'It didn't mind. It was *dead*.'

'But what did you do with him after?'

'I threw it out in the garden, of course.'

'Oh, *Halloran*!'

I saw the sudden falling flash of soft fat glimmering belly and scales, and heard the rustle of leaves where he landed. My eyes welled up in a blur.

'Oh, Christ,' said Halloran. 'You're going to be a farmer! Grow up! Even Cass doesn't fuss like this any more.'

I gave him a very sour look, and as I turned my head away again, he caught my chin in his firm long fingers. For one awful moment I thought he was going to kiss me, but he was only tipping my head back further into the light.

'You've changed,' he said. 'She told me you had.'

I jerked myself out of his grip.

'I want to talk to her. That's why I came.'

'She won't come out. She doesn't want to talk to you. She says she's still too upset.'

'You talk to her then. You tell her I'm sorry.'

'I've told her. That's what I've been doing.'

'Well, go back and tell her all over again!'

'If you like.'

He strolled back into the kitchen.

'All right, Plum?' I heard his voice come muffled back through the frosted-glass door. 'Find any nice chocolate ones in the tins? Tom still wants to talk to you, you know, Plumkin. Poor soul, he *is* in a state . . .'

I stuck my fingers in my ears. I didn't want to hear it. I couldn't bear to know that these gentle, animal-handling, panicky colt soothing noises were all laid on on my behalf because, left alone, I'd muff things up as usual. Plum, Halloran had called her. Plumkin! If he could call that sister of mine Plumkin and still get out of his kitchen alive, he could probably handle a viper. The only thing a clod like me could try a name like that on was one of the moles that were already dead in Jamieson's horrible bucket.

I couldn't stand it. It's bad enough being clumsy and stupid. I wasn't going to take on guilty as well. Furious, I scrambled to my feet.

'I'm sick of being in the wrong,' I yelled at her through the kitchen door. '*Sick* of it, do you hear me? And I don't care if you're still upset. I'm upset too, you know. But I'm not hanging around any more. I'm sorry. I'm sorry! I'm *sorry*! There! Now I've said it, and I'm not going to say it again. So if you want me never to speak to you again, you stay in there. And if you don't, you'd better come out quickly and say so!'

I didn't dare stay, in case she didn't come out. Jamming my muddy shoes on, I ran. And as I vaulted over his gate, I heard Halloran yelling, 'Bravo, Tom!' after me, through the rain.

Chapter 9

I told you, running's the one thing I've always done easily, better than Cass. And I only slowed up once, in spite of the wind and the rain that was driving in sheets full force into my face, and that was when I came round a bend and skidded to a halt behind Jamieson.

There he was, reeling unsteadily down the very same footpath. I guessed he'd come this way because it goes down to the short cut over the bridge; but he was hours late as it was, and I knew the moment Dad caught him swaying, or noticed that give-away bottle bulge in his work-jacket pocket, he was more likely to give him the sack than let him loose on the farm work.

I sheered off the path. I'm used to avoiding Jamieson whenever I can, but only since Lisa left and he fell apart like this had I felt so rotten and responsible that, rather than simply run past him on some narrow footpath, I'd take off round the edge of a field in weather like that.

He didn't notice, I'm sure. The rain would have stung and blinded a bull. He couldn't have heard me scrambling over the gate. I hardly heard myself. The wind, hurling round and round in the treetops, then shrilling down to buffet my ears and shriek up again, was just as deafening for him as for me. I floundered on through mud and slapping wet grasses, and twice nearly slipped in the drainage ditch I'd cleared with Dad, where frothy grey whirlpools were spinning along to the swollen river.

The crops were lashed flat. Even the tops of the sturdy hedges I followed were whipped dead level by squalling winds. The branches of the trees I passed swarmed down towards me, creaking horribly, like spooks thrusting out at a ghost train.

Gales frighten me. I hate high winds. I hate to see trees I know forced to bend, and bend further, till I've caught my breath in horror, certain the trunk can't give any more, will crack and split, and let that vast heavy wet-leafed mass above topple and crash. I've hated high winds ever since that seagull landed in Jamieson's garden, and all this other hating around me began. But I felt uneasy about them long before that. I've felt uneasy since the storm night Cass and I watched together through dark rain-streaked panes, as the comfortable, nest-ridden tree outside the window of the room we still shared was battered into one horrible unrecognizable black wet shape after another, and I heard each swelling creak and strain as a real feeling groan.

'It won't break.' I plucked at my pyjamas anxiously and told myself over and over: 'It won't break. It won't.'

I didn't really believe it, and I didn't whisper it softly enough.

'It will,' Cass said. And with a pistol-shot crack, the closest heavy heaving branch outside snapped like a twig. Now, looking back, I see again the brittle shredding black bark and all that floury fluffy maggot-white pulp spilling out on the grass, and I know that branch was dead wood. But way back then, and for years afterwards, I thought that Cass had made it happen.

I'm not a baby any more. I can work right

through a gale if I have to. I don't like them, though, and that's why, when I reached the edge of the spinney, I turned aside and made for the ice house instead of keeping on the path to the farm. I jerked back the sodden bramble wall and showers of droplets splattered up in my face. They blinded me for a moment, so I didn't see Cass sitting waiting, her long legs out-stretched, inside the tunnel entrance.

I stumbled over her, and fell, cracking my head hard against the tunnel wall, and sprawling head-long in the mud.

She pulled her legs out from under me so sharply a buckle on her shoe caught in my jacket. I tried to help in the untangling, but my fall hurt so much I ended up leaning against the tunnel brickwork more because she had shoved me back there than through any efforts of my own. I rubbed my head, panting, while she unhooked herself from me by wrenching out one of my buttons.

She didn't speak, and I sat forcing the tears back until the pain had subsided enough for me to open my eyes again.

She was looking at me with disgust and contempt.

'It *hurt*,' I said, our old ritual saying for getting observed tears honourably discounted.

The moment I said it I wished I hadn't. It sounded silly and weak and childish. I can cry if I bloody well feel like it.

The scornful look on her face didn't alter. I felt an anger rise in me from deep down inside, a terrible anger with my sister, Cass, for being there in the tunnel at all, for always being there to see my tears, for never missing any of my daily humiliations. Why hadn't she run on to the farm? How had she known I'd turn aside at the spinney, to come down here? Why should she know so much about me? I don't want anyone to know me that well, down to the very things that frighten me, and where I'll run to escape them. I want to have my secrets, like Lisa. I don't want to have a twin any more and I don't want to be one.

The anger didn't last. I rubbed my head and rubbed my knee and waited, and soon that old familiar sense of defeat welled up and took over, that old old feeling that Cass can do anything better than I can, anything she wants. Just look. I was supposed to be the faster runner. It's the only thing I have, after all. But one small detour of mine round a field was all it had taken for her to get here before me.

I slumped back against the brickwork, still panting, to hide my humiliation.

'You didn't waste much time,' I told her and added, to keep my end up, 'Plumkin.'

For someone who'd hurried over here to bury the hatchet, she didn't look any too friendly. And even 'Plumkin' didn't make her smile. You'd think from the way she stared at me, she'd never heard the name before in her life.

'You've been a rotten brother, Tom! *Rotten!*'

I stared back at her, not understanding at all. Her cry swung round and round and round at me. *Rotten! Rotten! Rotten! Rotten!* Rather than weaken, the echo seemed to grow in force and fury. Her face was ugly in the green half-light, distorted with rage. She was painfully twisting her long slim fingers. They writhed like the worms in Jamieson's bucket. I've never seen real hands wringing before. It was horrible.

'Cass—'

But she had already jumped to her feet.

'I'm sick of you!' she shouted in my face. 'Sick of you, do you hear me? Sick of your endless watching and waiting. Sick of your wondering about me. You've got to stop! Stop all the following! With you around I don't feel whole. You're everywhere. You're in my skin! You have to let me go, Tom. Can you understand that? Let go of me! Let me *go*!'

She hit out at the hand I laid on her arm, to try and stop her. She hit hard, and pushing me violently, she ran off out of the ice house.

I let my hand fall. The wind outside dropped momentarily, and through the sudden un-expected calm I heard her crashing down through the undergrowth, and, as I listened, from the river came a short high creak and a splintering crash, then an almighty splash, as if at the same time something else outside, like Cass and me, was being broken up for ever.

I stood up and shook myself like a dog. I stumbled down the tunnel into the dome, groping about in my pockets for matches. I struck one, and only when its feeble wavering light filled out and steadied did I see the egg book lying muddied and broken-spined on the floor, where she must have hurled it the moment she heard me returning.

'I'm warning you, Tom,' she'd said to me that morning. 'I'm not the only one with secrets round here, and I'll pay you back!'

I hadn't followed her to Halloran's at all. She'd followed me. She'd followed me down here, and stayed out of sight till I'd gone off, then she'd slipped in and prised up the bricks and unwrapped the tin foil in search of her stolen door key. The egg book must have fallen open, and she'd sat reading all I'd written here in the back, every word, the whole story, while I, like the idiot I am, had gone off after her to Halloran's place. I'd stared at drawings of Lisa's hands pointing and stroking and wringing, and making finger steeples in the air, and even at a painting of her unmistakable thin crooked fingers – so unlike anyone else's that Halloran had wanted them especially – and still I hadn't had the sense to realize that it was Lisa in the kitchen with Halloran. Lisa, not Cass. It wasn't my sister I'd yelled at so furiously through the door. It was Lisa. Cass had been here the whole time. She'd been here reading. She'd read everything I wrote about Lisa, down to my most secret daydreams. She'd read everything I wrote about her, how I'd nosed and poked through the things in her room. She'd read all the nasty things Jamieson hinted about her.

Jamieson! Whom I'd last seen staggering down the short cut to the old bridge! I heard again that creak and splintering crash and the splash, but this time the creak sounded different to me, more like what it must have been – his cracked and drunken screech of terror as rotten boards were giving beneath him.

I shook the match out and ran, and even before I reached the bank I heard above the wind the short sharp barks of his cries for help as he floundered deep in the flooding river.

The force and the cold of the water had shocked him right out of the state he'd been in, for now he was flailing about like a madman and staying afloat, though he can't swim a stroke, by sheer massive desperate effort. He seemed to be getting somewhere. As I kicked off my shoes he seemed to work himself out of the worst of the current and struggle closer to the bank. It looked as if he might make it.

I took off my jacket and both my sweaters, but I didn't dive in and try and save him. Like Cass,

standing set-faced watching him further along,
I waited to see if he'd manage alone. I know how
strong he is. I've seen him lift bales. The way he
was panicking, I couldn't rescue him. He would
drown me and, clinging to me, he would drown
that much quicker himself.

His arms thrashed like berserk waterwheels. I
watched him struggle and flail his way closer and
closer through the surging water, until one
desperate hand grasped far enough to clutch at a
clump of dark slithery reeds at Cass's feet.

She didn't make a move to help him. She didn't
even put out her hand. She stood there as if
she were paralysed, while he pulled and pulled
at the reeds till he was so close his feet touched
the riverbed underneath him at last, and he began
to heave himself out of the water.

He reared up in front of her, shaking and
swaying, a huge grey dripping sodden mass, like
some enormous mouldering corpse clambering
out of a grave. Reaching forward, he suddenly
grabbed her.

And then Cass moved. But not to help him.
The moment he touched her she panicked, she
must have, because she suddenly kicked out at

him as he struggled out of the water in front of her. She picked at his scrabbling clawing fingers, stamped with her shoes on his frantic hands, and when he still kept coming, threw herself at him and tried to push his fear-ugly soaking face out and away from her, backwards.

He groaned and roared, but she kept pushing and kicking at every bit of him that rose out of the water at her. She struggled with him like a wild cat, prising his wet fingers from her clothing, forcing him back, until in desperation and terror she kicked at him one time too many, too hard, and he arched back, his arms splayed out, his whole face contorted. Blood from his nose splurted over the grass and her shoes and the water, and by the time I reached her and jerked her safely away from the edge, she had shovelled the huge shapeless bulk of him back in the river. I couldn't believe it. She'd pushed him back in there. Cass had pushed and kicked him back in!

His body started to sink. But then his ballooning jacket swung him round and over. He swept right past us, exhausted and bleeding, and trapped once again in the current.

I ran along the bank so fast I reached the

landing-stage well before he did. I kneeled against the outermost post, and pushing my sodden hair back out of my eyes, reached out for him as he came closer. His eyes rolled and his face shone with effort. He grabbed out wildly towards me.

I leaned as far as I dared out over the water.

'Come on!' I yelled at him. 'Try to *swim*, Jamieson! *Try!* Try *swimming*, Jamieson! *Please!*'

He couldn't possibly have heard what I said in that wind with all that water tumbling around him; but my shouting seemed to give him strength to keep going, and thrusting and splashing he thrashed his way closer and closer towards me.

I leaned so far over I almost fell in. I reached my arms out to him. 'Come *on*, Jamieson!' I shouted. '*Kick*, will you? *Kick!*'

He kicked and kicked, and forced himself on until my fingers almost touched his. The boards beneath shook my knees as Cass ran up behind me. I felt her arm slide round my waist and grip me, and when she'd anchored her other arm safely around the wooden post beside us, I managed to lean so much further forward that I caught his weakening fingers.

The current tore him away at once, but as he swirled past me I caught at his hand again, firmer this time, enough to hold on. Cass hauled me back with all her strength, and I hauled him, the whole sodden weight of him, through the strong current.

Together we pulled him back to the edge.

His face was so close I was breathing his breath. We pulled him up alongside the landing-stage as if he were some dead whale we'd caught. I had my arms around him.

'Up!' I hissed in his ear. 'Come *on*, Jamieson! *Up!*'

I've never lifted anything so heavy. We strained and pulled to try and heave him up over the edge. Halfway we let him slip a little, and panicking he reached out wildly and grabbed a fistful of Cass's hair. I heard it squeaking as he pulled himself up, but neither of us let go of him till he was safely up on the boards.

Cass couldn't see to free herself. She crouched beside him, her eyes filled with tears, until I'd disentangled his stiff clutching fingers.

I reached down to lever his legs up from where they still dangled in the water. Together we rolled him further away from the edge, and he lay groaning face down on the boards, while Cass and I leaned back against the posts, gasping.

I wiped the sweat out of my eyes. Cass looked chalk-white and exhausted.

'I'll fetch some help,' I told her.

Opening her eyes, she looked down at Jamieson, horrified.

'I'll go, Tom. Please.'

She didn't want to be left alone with him, I could tell. Suppose he needed touching, or comfort. It wasn't so long since I myself had first seen him close to tears beside his fruit bushes that I'd had time to forget quite how it feels. I felt so sorry for Cass. I'd rather see someone I love in that state than someone I hated. At least you could reach out and touch them. You wouldn't have to just stand there and watch. Poor Cass has loathed Jamieson so long, how could she bear to see him lying there so suddenly, shivering with cold and fear and too much drink, bedraggled and helpless, like some gigantic mole tipped carelessly out of his very own bucket.

'Go on then, Cass. You go.'

I stretched my hand towards her, and she held

it tightly as she stumbled to her feet. She padded off unsteadily over the boards. I waited till she'd disappeared between the trees, and then I shook enough sense back into Jamieson to get him to stand. I fetched my jacket to drape round his shoulders, and holding him close, I led him off the landing-stage and up the slope to the ice house, out of the wind as if he were half blind or simple.

And that's where Lisa found me, soon after-wards, pale from her run from Halloran's, and paler still when she saw the two of us together, propped up against the brickwork, leaning against one another for warmth. She took her father's hand and I took hers, and we waited quietly till Dad came down with brandy, and tea in flasks, and blankets, and cursing Jamieson for a fool and a drunk, led him back up the path to the farmhouse.

Before we left to follow them, I carefully prised the tell-tale unused bus ticket to Lincoln out from between her nervous fingers, where she'd been shredding its edges.

'You didn't go, then.'

She shook her head.

'Halloran simply took you off the bus, didn't he?'

She nodded.

'You didn't even argue.'

She didn't even argue. She probably didn't even care. I bet she just stepped off the bus with him without thinking twice. She wouldn't care one way or the other if she spent the week sitting still on a stool with her hands in her lap for Halloran, or visiting her Aunt Bridget in Lincoln. You couldn't call it kidnapping (though Dad will if ever he gets to hear of it). It's just Lisa all over. She's like that.

She'll get away with it, I'm sure. I doubt if Dad thought twice about her sudden reappearance, and Jamieson wasn't thinking at all. Aunt Bridget won't use the telephone. She's been deaf for years. But when she writes to mention how long it's been since she has seen her niece, Lisa will simply skip that bit out when she reads the letter aloud to her father. No doubt she and Halloran between them will forge some suitable reply, under which Jamieson will, all unknowing, scrawl his unhandy signature.

I felt tired and angry when I looked at her. It

bothers me, the way she doesn't care. It doesn't make the slightest difference to my feelings – believe me, I've tried that – but I'd feel so much easier about those feelings if Lisa were different. I wish at times that she were more like Cass. At least my sister goes after the things that she cares about, and goes after them hard. I sometimes wonder whether Lisa will ever care very much about anything.

I handed back the bus ticket to Lincoln.

'You really ought to burn this,' I warned.

I struck a match. She held the bus ticket out over the flame, and as the paper flared up and filled the ice house with light, she reached down for the egg book which still lay, tattered and muddy, upon the floor.

'What's this, Tom?'

'Nothing. A list, mostly.'

'A list of what?'

I didn't answer, and after a moment she carried it to the tunnel entrance. '"*Clumsy*",' she read out '"*Stupid, rude, awkward, prickly, sullen . . .*" What is this, Tom?'

I shrugged and looked away, embarrassed.

'A list of faults.'

'Whose faults?'

'Mine. Mine and Cass's. Cass's and mine.'

Shuddering, she dropped the egg book back in the mud. 'You ought to burn that, too, then,' she said.

Chapter 10

She's right. I lay awake last night and thought about it, and she's quite right. I ought to burn The List. That's all it's fit for. I came down here this morning and felt a wave of anger just flicking back through it, page after page of insults. Insults, nothing but insults. Our weaknesses are scattered through like peppergrains. *Hot-tempered* – is that Cass's fault? *Slow* – is that mine?

I hate The List. I *hate* it. Why have I carried on with it so long? I should have torn it up months ago and argued back at them, like Cass does. I thought, before, she'd won her battles easily, like she does everything. But now, as I look back through the egg book, I see just how hard it's been for her. *Insolents* and *defiants*, *obstinates* and *difficults*, *awkwards* and *irritatings*. They litter the last twenty pages. With all this going on every day, no wonder she lost interest in keeping The List.

She's coming through, though, I can tell. If they say anything to her: 'Cass! It's so *thoughtless* of you to leave things lying about your room for someone else to pick up!' then Cass is right back in there, fighting. 'I don't see why. It's my room, isn't it? I clean it up when I think it needs it. I don't ask anyone else to clean it up for me.' And now they don't tangle with her half as much over the silly little things. She keeps her room the way she wants. She wears what she chooses. She does what she believes in. She's slowly getting to live her own life.

But me? I've taken it. I've stood there silently, and let the things they've said hover round me, staining the very air I'm trying to breathe, until I've slunk down here to this damp miserable hole in the ground, to write them down in an egg book.

And up till now, it's worked, I suppose. That's why I kept it going alone. The List has kept them all for me, failings and insults and weaknesses, held them like black gassed moths pinned in neat rows. They couldn't rise and flap around my head once they'd been written down on The List.

But it's no use any longer. There's no point in my keeping it now. I know now that the things people say about me can't be pinned down like dried dead moths. I can't write those things Cass said about me away, just as she can't take back having said them. They'll hover round my head for ever unless I know for certain that they're not true any longer.

So I'm going to change, like Cass. For me it will be harder. It always is. But I shall manage it, I'm sure I shall, so sure I gave Cass her door key back yesterday in return for a smile, and today I'm going to burn up The List as a sign there'll be no going backwards, not ever. All this I've written in the back will have to go too, but that doesn't matter. There was no more to tell in any case.

I've brought down one last candle. I'm going to hold the pages up in its flame, one by one. The thin grey paper will glow a warm friendly pink in the light. I'll wait a moment, and then the fuzzy torn-off edge will blacken suddenly, as if by magic, and streaks of earth-brown will flare across, obliterating the writing and those cold steadfast horrid pale blue lines that seem to say: *This paper's not for pleasure. Mind you use this for copying French exercises, or ordering eggs, or keeping a list of your failings. It's not for you to use for anything else, like drawing the pale peaky face of someone you're thinking about, or writing your name and weaving colourful patterns around every letter.*

The page will catch fire. Tendrils of fine grey smoke will curl in the air and those rich golden blue-based flames will swoop up into life, and make me twist the paper smartly around in my fingers. That dark, dark marching burn, with its distinctive cleansing smell, like brushwood burning after years and years, will move across the paper, seizing it up and shrinking it, until the heat upon my fingertips forces me into letting go and dropping it on the tin foil beside me.

I'll watch it glow that vivid spluttering orange, then crumple and blacken and cool. I'll blow the frail remains away across the ice-house floor. Perhaps they'll rustle faintly in protest, like last year's dead leaves. Then I'll rip out another page, and another, and so get rid of all of them for ever.

When I've burned up the egg book, I'll start on

the huge silver scrapbook, where it began. I'll burn it page by page, from back to front, through all the failings and weaknesses and faults. I'll burn up years and years. I'll see the words we wrote in careful columns down each of its grey spongy pages, but I won't be reading them. Like Cass, I'm through with it all. I'll watch the shadows moving over the brickwork, a feverish dance of farewell for every page, but I'll be thinking of other things.

The cover will be hard to burn. It's still as stiff and shiny and bright as when Aunt Nina gave it to us, so long ago. She'd be amazed to know we'd kept it, and kept it so well. That's going, too, though. The thin silver coating will warp and shrivel and blister, and separate from its tough cardboard backing. I'll probably scorch my fingers burning that, but then at last The List will be gone.

I'll look down at the two bricks we kept it under for so long, and I'll know it's not there any more. Cass? She won't even notice it's gone. And I won't miss it. There's so much work to get through on the farm now poor old Jamieson's laid up for a while, I probably won't be coming down here much any more.

ABOUT THE AUTHOR

Anne Fine was born in Leicester. She went to Wallisdean County Primary School in Fareham, Hampshire, and then to Northampton High School for Girls. She read Politics and History at the University of Warwick and then worked as an information officer for Oxfam before teaching (very briefly!) in a Scottish prison. She started her first book during a blizzard that stopped her getting to Edinburgh City Library and has been writing ever since.

Anne Fine is now a hugely popular and celebrated author. Among the many awards she has won are the Carnegie Medal (twice), the Whitbread Children's Novel Award (twice), the Guardian Children's Literature Award and a Smarties Prize. She has twice been voted Children's Writer of the Year at the British Book Awards and was the Children's Laureate for 2001-2003.

She has written over forty books for young people, including *Goggle-Eyes*, *Flour Babies*, *Bill's New Frock*, *The Tulip Touch* and *Madame Doubtfire*. She has also written a number of titles for adult readers, and has edited three poetry collections.

Anne Fine lives in County Durham and has two daughters and a large hairy dog called Harvey.

www.annefine.co.uk

ANNE FINE

Up on Cloud Nine

**How stupid do you have to be to fall out of
a top-floor window.**

Or was Stolly trying something else?
Up on cloud nine.
It's up to his best mate, Ian, to find out the truth...

HIGHLY COMMENDED FOR THE CARNEGIE
MEDAL

'Anne Fine on top form' OBSERVER

'[A] brave and sometimes brilliant book' INDEPENDENT

'A tour de force – moving, funny, pacey and
profound' GUARDIAN

'Subtle and entertaining...will make children of
both sexes accept unusualness and difference, both
in themselves and in others' SUNDAY TIMES

0 552 54840 5

www.kidsatrandomhouse.co.uk

aNNE FINE

The Granny Project

Blackmail – or negotiation?

Mum and Dad reckon things would be better if
Granny were in a Home.
The kids all want her to stay.
Ivan's Granny Project should make his parents
think again.
But there's more than one way of doing a project –
and blackmail can work two ways...

A savagely funny tale from multi-award-winning
author Anne Fine.

Shortlisted for the Guardian Children's Fiction
Award.

'Clever, funny and thoughtful' TLS

'Both audacious and heart-warming' NEW STATESMAN

0 552 55438 3

www.kidsatrandomhouse.co.uk